"Chung-Cha belongs to Christ," Father declared. "Even if you destroy me, God will still watch over my daughter."

The agent chuckled.

"And what if I destroy her?"

Praise for *The Beloved Daughter* by Alana Terry

Grace Awards, First Place

IndieFab Finalist, Religious Fiction

Women of Faith Writing Contest, Second Place

Book Club Network Book of the Month, First Place

Reader's Favorite Gold Medal, Christian Fiction

"...an engaging plot that reads like a story out of today's headlines..." ~ *Women of Faith Writing Contest*

"In this meticulously researched novel, Terry gives readers everything a good novel should have — a gripping story, an uplifting theme, encouragement in their own faith, and exquisite writing." ~ *Grace Awards Judges' Panel*

"The Beloved Daughter is a beautifully written story." ~ Sarah Palmer, Liberty in North Korea

The Beloved Daughter

Daughter

a novel by Alana Terry

Also available in ebook and audiobook formats.
www.alanaterry.com

To my precious Ae-Cha,
so you will always know that you are
my beloved daughter.

CHARACTER'S NAMES AND MEANINGS

Female Characters
Chung-Cha: *Righteous daughter*
Choon-Hee: *Spring maiden*
Mee-Kyong: *Bright and beautiful*
Kyung-Soon: *Gentleness and peace*
So-Young: *Eternal beauty*

Male Characters
Hyun-Ki: *Foundation of wisdom*
Chul-Moo: *Weapon of iron*
Chung-Ho: *Righteous and good*
Shin: *Faith*
Kwan: *Strength*

Historical Characters
Kim Jong-Il: also known as "the Dear Leader,"
the General and Supreme Commander of North Korea
during the events of this book

PART ONE

Hasambong
North Hamyong Province
North Korea
1998

A BRUISED REED

"A bruised reed he will not break, and a smoldering wick he will not snuff out." Isaiah 42:3

"Are you trying to get us all killed with your recklessness? These inspectors report directly to Pyongyang."

The wind howled as gusts of snow burst through the cracks in our cabin walls. If the stinging cold and the hunger pains weren't already keeping me awake, my parents' hushed argument would be. I hugged my blanket as I listened to their voices, forceful and angry as the winter gale.

I slipped one eye open, just a crack. My parents stood in the middle of our cabin facing each other. Father didn't move at all. His face reminded me of the statue of our nation's founder in front of our school. Kim Il-Sung's bronze image never yielded in rain or snow but gazed resolutely at his starving citizens with cold and stony eyes.

"I will not renounce the truths of Scripture just to make my life here on this earth more comfortable," Father spat. He was still whispering, but the forcefulness of his words filled our cabin like the roar of the angry Tumen River in flood season. "'If you falter in times of trouble,'" Father quoted, "'how small is your strength'!"

Mother swore. "Don't talk to me about *strength*! Don't you think I wish things were different? But they're not. You think I'm a coward. But I'm the one who watches out for our daughter's safety while you bring open suspicion upon our household right in front of the inspectors. No, Husband." Mother pointed a finger in his face. "It is you who are the coward."

I longed to rush to Father's aid. In the candlelight, I saw Father's frame droop. His shoulders sagged. I waited for Father to respond, willing him to defend himself, but he was silent.

2

"You dare speak to me about courage." I wondered if Mother knew she was shouting now. "You don't realize how much *courage* it takes to get up every morning and go to work, knowing that my daughter could be interrogated any day by her teachers at that school. Knowing that I'm powerless to worship God like the Good Book says if I want my only child to see her thirteenth birthday. Knowing that my husband thinks I'm an apostate because I would rather see Chung-Cha survive to adulthood. And meanwhile you – for the sake of a mere philosophy – are willing to condemn our entire family to prison camp. Of course you realize what those guards would do to Chung-Cha there, don't you?" I prayed for sleep to shield me from my mother's words.

"And do you know what will happen to Chung-Cha if she dies without ever learning the good news?" Father whispered.

"She *knows* the good news. Why isn't that enough? Why do you continue to endanger our only child? Especially now with the inspectors here, looking to make an example of traitors?"

"The Lord will care for us." I pretended not to hear the strain in Father's voice.

"You are certain of God's provision," Mother countered. "Yet if Chung-Cha doesn't die of cold and hunger this winter, she'll just as likely die in a prison camp this spring. All because of your recklessness. You have the word of God in your heart. Why can't you keep it there instead of speaking so openly and condemning us all?"

Father was speechless. I willed away the sob that was rising in my throat at the sight of my dear father so humiliated. Could Mother be right? I had never met anyone like my father. He memorized whole books of the Bible although Scripture was outlawed in North Korea. He shared the gospel with his co-workers although it was dangerous. Father's faith was so strong that I was certain the Hasambong mountains themselves would one day cave in at the sound of his prayers breathed in the darkness. Could this man really be wrong to love God so deeply? Was Father foolish to obey God so fearlessly?

Father always promised that God would care for us just like he cared for the sparrows. Years ago, I was quick and eager to believe Father's words of faith. But as each month of the famine grew worse, as each night I shivered from the cold and clenched my empty stomach while listening in on my parents' disagreements, I wondered if my mother could be right. Seeds of doubt found fertile soil in my empty belly.

In our Hasambong village, even the sparrows were dying from hunger.

Now with the inspectors here, the danger was even more real. The prison camps weren't just rumors. Two families in our small village of Hasambong had been relocated since the start of the famine. One couple was caught with a stolen potato. The other family, whose infant I played with before she starved to death, was accused of cannibalism.

Was Mother right? With the People's Safety Agency here to inspect us, wouldn't God understand if Father was less vocal about his faith, given the circumstances and grave dangers to our family?

My father sighed, and I held my breath to hear what he would say in his defense. "I am not a fool. I know what risks come from following Jesus Christ." Father's voice wasn't angry anymore, but gentle, like the snow that occasionally covered the Hasambong mountainside in a blanket of unblemished white. "Chung-Cha is a gift from God ... as are you." Father reached out his calloused, work-worn hand to wipe a tear off Mother's gaunt cheek. She turned away with a disdainful snort.

Father continued, "Nevertheless, if I begin to love these gifts more than the One who entrusted them to me, then I would not

4

be able to look my Savior in the face when I stand before him and give an account of my life. It is God who gives me breath." The confidence of Father's quiet confession filled our cabin with uncharacteristic warmth. "And as long as my old worn-out heart keeps beating, as long as these tired lungs continue to draw air, I will not remain silent. I cannot. I will proclaim the Good News until my Savior returns to rule the earth or until he calls me home."

My heart swelled at Father's words of triumph and faith. I watched Mother's face to see if she felt the same wave of power, the same surge of hope, that transcended the suffering and fear – even the constant hunger – of our provincial lives in rural North Korea.

Mother brushed past Father and unpinned her hair. She walked to the bed, yanked down the tattered blanket, and hissed, "Your stubborn faith will be the death of us all."

THE TEST

*"But Peter insisted emphatically, 'Even if I have to die with you,
I will never disown you.'" Mark 14:31*

Inspectors stormed into our cabin less than an hour later.

"Get up!" a raspy voice demanded as several men crashed
the door in. Snow blew all the way to my bedside. Partially
blinded by the flashlights, I was too stunned to even tremble.

Is this part of the inspection? I wondered. *Are they going to
interrogate us here?* Mother moaned. I peeked from under the
blanket to see her wrapping Father's coat around his shoulders.
Where does she think he'll be going on a night like this?

A man with dozens of pock-mark scars on his face
stomped toward my parents' bed. He wore the badge of the
People's Safety Agency on his dark green overcoat. His heavy
boots shook the floor with each stride. When he grabbed Father
by the neck and yanked him out of bed, I yelped like a
wounded animal.

The scar-faced man turned on his heel without letting go of
my father and pointed at me. "The girl," Pock-Marks ordered in
a hoarse rasp, and immediately two officers towered over me. I
bit my lip to keep from crying when I saw the guns swinging
from their hips. I covered my face with my hands, trying to
disappear by sheer force of will. I squeaked my protests as the
younger of the two officers lifted me up and swung me over his
shoulder so that I was hanging down over his back. Mother ran
toward them with my coat, but they ignored both her pathetic
pleading and my frantic kicking.

"Take her to the precinct building," instructed the scar-faced
leader, and before I had time to call out again, my abductor
carried me outside into the snowy darkness. Still in my

nightgown, with no shoes or coat or blanket to ward off the biting cold, I hung over the young officer's shoulder.

I strained my neck and saw Father standing in the doorway as soldiers roughly shoved him forward. He winced as the inspectors fastened his wrists, and then he turned to see me watching him. Weakly, Father smiled at me, nodding his head in my direction. As the officer carrying me rounded a sharp corner, I clung desperately to that last image of Father.

In spite of my fears, I was relieved when we entered the precinct building. It wasn't much warmer than the outside, but at least it was protected from the wind and snow. My heart sank just as quickly, however, when I saw that there was no one else there. When the People's Safety agents first entered into our home, I forced myself to believe that their visit was all a routine part of the inspection. As I was being carried to the precinct building, I told myself that once we got there I would see other children like myself, all huddled and waiting together for some mass demonstration.

Instead I was alone in the dark building with no parents, no familiar faces, only my two captors. My family was being singled out. Is this why Mother begged Father not to draw attention to us? What other reason could there be – besides Father's faith – to explain why I was here right now, wet from the snow and shivering in a dark and unheated room?

My abductor dropped me onto the hard floor in a corner and talked in a whisper to his partner. After a moment, the older officer rubbed his hands together and stepped back out into the snow, leaving me and the other guard alone. The young inspection officer stood for a while at attention and then finally sat down in a chair by the door and fidgeted with a pocketknife.

I waited for something to happen: for my parents to join me, for the guard to say something. Nothing. There was only quietness and darkness and fear. I knew what Father would do in my place; he would pray. But I never could pray like Father, and I didn't have any proof that God listened to me or felt like intervening on my behalf anyway.

When I was twelve, you see, my father's faith was so strong that it seemed completely unattainable. I could never be as steadfast or as bold as he, not while I was still so young. Fervent faith was reserved for adults like my father – a grown man who had over half of the New Testament memorized – or like the Bible smuggler who risked his own life to give Father his illegal copy of Scripture.

Huddled in the dark corner of the precinct building, I thought about the stories I knew about this Christian worker. He was known only by his alias, Moses. A Chinese citizen of Korean ethnicity, Moses was wanted at great price by both the Chinese and North Korean police. In addition to smuggling Bibles into our starving land, Moses had also helped dozens of Koreans find safe passage into China. According to rumors, he could even warn Christian leaders of imminent arrests and somehow usher them to safety across the border.

Moses' very existence was enigmatic. How did a Chinese citizen know enough about the inner workings of Pyongyang that he could save Christians from impending raids? How could a foreigner orchestrate the release of condemned Korean church leaders? How could a mortal man slip from country to country without getting caught by either the Koreans or Chinese?

I probably wouldn't have believed half of these legends at all if Father didn't know Moses personally. As I squatted on the floor in the precinct building, I wondered what Moses was doing right now. Did he remember Father, the man from Hasambong he gave a Bible to so many years ago? Did Moses know about me at all? Did Moses pray for Hyun-Ki's only child, Chung-Cha? Most importantly, did Moses have a plan to rescue our family?

In spite of my hopeless circumstances, my heart raced in excitement. Was this entire abduction one of Moses' feats of deliverance? Would the Bible smuggler himself show up and whisk my parents and me away to safety? To freedom?

From the corner of my eye, I studied the young agent who sat by the door guarding me. Face taut, body slouched in his chair, he twiddled his pocketknife with a bored expression. He caught me staring at him and spat at the spot on the floor where I crouched. As hard as I tried, I couldn't believe that he was an undercover Christian worker. He was a guard from the inspection unit of the People's Safety Agency. Nothing more. And my detainment here was not a regular aspect of the inspection rounds either.

My teeth were clicking from the cold, but I didn't ask my captor for a blanket. The metal stove in the middle of the room remained unlit. I sat against the wall and hugged my legs, waiting for Mother and Father to arrive, trying against all logic to hold on to my quickly fading dreams of Moses and freedom.

I don't know how long I sat there in the cold and the dark, but eventually I heard footsteps marching down the outer hallway. The guard who was supposed to be watching me was dozing in his chair. As the footsteps grew louder, he jumped up and straightened his hat and his uniform. He barely managed to get upright at attention before the heavy door swung open, letting in a gust of icy wind.

The pock-marked officer was the first to enter, followed by several other inspectors. One of the guards carried a lantern, and he placed it on a desk in the middle of the room. The flames flickered and danced. I shuddered and stared at the six pairs of snowy boots in front of me.

"Bring the woman here!" shouted Pock-Marks who wheezed when he spoke as if unseen hands were wrapping ghoulish fingers around his throat. I looked up and saw Mother standing in the shadows. At first I wanted to jump up and run to her, but I stopped and sucked in my breath when I saw her face. Her eyes were downcast, her expression vacant. The guard leading her pushed her through the door. Crude wire bound her wrists.

The guard shoved Mother before the scar-faced official. Her threadbare coat remained only halfway buttoned over her nightclothes, and her graying hair was disheveled and tangled from the wind. She didn't look at me even once but stared down at the officer's feet.

"Name!" Pock-Marks demanded, his voice so hoarse that I wished to cough for him.

"Lyang Choon-Hee," Mother answered.

I'm down here, Mother! I willed my thoughts to reach her, but she didn't look my way.

"Religion?" Pock-Marks inquired. He towered at least a head higher than Mother who stood before him with her shoulders slumped down.

"Religion!" he boomed once more, holding his pistol as if he was about to strike her with it. I turned my face away so that I wouldn't see the blow.

"I am a daughter of the Party," Mother answered, never raising her gaze. Pock-Marks lowered his weapon. Before returning it to its holster, however, he hesitated. Through the flickering lamplight I saw the corners of his lips turn upward into a twisted grin. He gestured to one of his companions and jerked his chin toward me. The man lifted me up and shoved me forward. Pock-Marks grabbed me by the shoulder and positioned me in front of my mother.

"Are the members of your family Christian pigs?" Pock-Marks asked, digging his fingernails into my neck.

"We are children of the Party," Mother replied.

Pock-Marks raised his hand again and hit her cheek with the butt of his pistol. I jumped and bit my lip to keep from crying out.

"Give me the truth," Pock-Marks ordered, "or else I'll crack open your daughter's skull." Mother tilted her head to the side and looked at me for the first time. She raised her eyebrows. When Pock-Marks lifted his gun over my head, Mother squared her shoulders and tilted her chin up.

"We are not Christians. We do not follow the ways of the Western deceiver Jesus."

"Do you swear it?"

Mother's voice was resolute, and she looked straight into the interrogator's eyes. "I swear it."

I gasped, terrified that God Almighty himself might smite my mother for her betrayal. I looked around for some sign of help but saw only the faces of half a dozen officers nodding at these words of apostasy.

Pock-Marks bent down so that his pitted face was only a few centimeters away from Mother's. Stuck between my mother and her interrogator, I had no way to fight the waves of horror that penetrated my very soul as he leaned against me. His uniform pressed into my back, and I could scarcely breathe.

"And what do you think of Christians?" The sweetness in Pock-Marks' voice made my head swirl.

Mother didn't pause for even a second. "They are pigs. They are illiterate, unintelligent swine who spit in the face of the Dear Leader in spite of all his goodness toward us. They don't deserve to be a part of this great nation, and the revolution would be better off if they were all drowned in the bottom of the sea."

I had never heard such words of blasphemy come from anyone's mouth, much less my own mother's. In my horror, I was certain I could now see demons dancing in the flickering lamplight. Pock-Marks grabbed my shoulders and spun me around to face him. His eyes were dark. I tried to turn away but couldn't. I stared into the officer's black irises, too petrified to move.

ALANA TERRY

"Remember this night," the wheezing officer instructed me, leaning so close to my face I could taste his putrid breath. I tried to break free from his stare, but I was paralyzed, whether from my own twelve-year-old fears or by the evil force that seemed to have grown exponentially at Mother's words of unfaithfulness.

Eventually, Pock-Marks released his hold on me and straightened up. "Take her away," Pock-Marks ordered a junior guard, who was only a few years older than I. The young man shoved Mother forward with a jerk and pushed her out of the room. She didn't even look back at me.

Pock-Marks turned toward his comrades. "The people of Hasambong told us she wouldn't be a problem." He shrugged. "It's the male that will require some extra persuasion." He looked at me and winked. I wanted to clasp my hands over my ears to try to block out the dark laughter that followed from his colleagues, but my limbs still refused to obey me.

"Bring in the traitor!" Pock-Marks shouted.

COURAGE TO STAND

"Strike the shepherd, and the sheep will be scattered."
Zechariah 13:7

Father stood in the doorway, bound like Mother but even more tightly. The cords around his wrists cut into his skin. Dried blood caked around his lip where it was split open. When he saw me, Father smiled faintly. His demeanor assured me; I didn't even cry out when the junior guard shoved Father so hard that he fell at Pock-Mark's feet by the metal stove in the middle of the room.

"Name," rasped the scar-faced interrogator.

"Song Hyun-Ki," replied Father as he stood up to face his accuser. *Remember the steadiness of Father's voice.* I forced myself to focus on Father's powerful presence. *Remember how calm he is. Remember the peace you feel right now.* It was a stark contrast to the cold of Pock-Marks's touch or the shock of my mother's apostasy just moments earlier.

"Religion?"

Father didn't hesitate. "I worship Jesus Christ, the risen Son of God, the Savior of all men."

On hearing Father's words, I was sure the officer would beat him, but for the slightest moment, a look of terror flashed through Pock-Marks' dark eyes. I was certain that Father noticed it as well, and he glanced in my direction as if to say, *Did you see it too, Daughter?*

Unfortunately, that moment of victory was fleeting. The officer looked Father up and down and then smiled. "It's a dangerous proposition," Pock-Marks goaded, "being so bold when there are children present."

I stood still, willing myself to breathe. The corner of Father's lip quivered, but his voice betrayed no terror as he spoke.

"Chung-Cha belongs to Christ," Father declared. "Even if you destroy me, God will still watch over my daughter."

The agent chuckled, taking a single stride toward me. "And what if I destroy her?" In one swift motion, Pock-Marks grabbed my hair and yanked me down until I was kneeling on the ground in front of the stove.

"Father!" I yelped. The officer could break my neck with one strong snap. I heard Father suck in his breath as if someone hit him straight in the gut.

"Answer me now, you filthy Christian pig." Pock-Marks was wheezing even as he sneered at Father. "Will you let your daughter suffer for the sake of this precious religion?"

Out of the corner of my eye, I saw Father set his jaw. "My daughter and I do not cower in fear of those who can harm the body but cannot kill the soul."

Pock-Marks pulled my head back even more and then slammed it hard against the metal stove. A loud crack sounded in my ears, and hot blood gushed from my forehead. My vision blurred. "Father!" I tried to cry out, but words wouldn't form. The sense of tranquility vanished, and only one thought remained:

This man was going to kill me.

The officer laughed. "This is how Christian pigs protect their offspring!" Pock-Marks pulled my head back again. I was going to die while my father stood by watching helplessly.

"Don't!" I croaked, finally finding my voice.

Pock-Marks laughed again. For a moment, my fear was replaced by anger toward Father and toward the God he served so faithfully, both of whom seemed so powerless at that moment to intervene on my behalf.

This time the officer slammed my entire face flat onto the stovetop. Blood spilled from my nose and choked me as it pooled in the back of my throat.

"What do you have to say for yourself now, fool?" Pock-Marks asked. "Only a stupid pig would serve an invisible god who can't save a little girl." The officer held my face back so Father could watch me trying to cough up blood. Father's voice betrayed his tears as he proclaimed, "The suffering that my family and I endure in this life is nothing compared to the hope that we have for the glorious kingdom of heaven. Our light and momentary trials are achieving for us an even greater reward."

"If you insist on serving your Western puppet god, I'll kill your daughter without the slightest regret," Pock-Marks snarled, his once-raspy voice now inexplicably clear as he slammed my face a third time onto the stovetop.

"My daughter belongs to Christ," Father announced, choking on his sob. Beloved daughter, I must confess to you that in that moment I hated Father for his stubborn faith. I couldn't keep my eyes open. Another blow and I would be dead.

Though crying, Father addressed me with surprising confidence. "Righteous daughter," he declared, loudly enough so that everyone could hear, "there is no shame in suffering for the gospel, only reward." His words sounded distant and fuzzy as my skull was bashed once more against the metallic edge of the stove.

"Jesus Christ also died at the hands of wicked men." Father was sobbing as he preached. Whether he was speaking to me, or my attacker, or the half a dozen men who stood by watching the violence unfold I didn't know. I didn't care, either. Father's words were meaningless. Pock-Marks meant to kill me. What good were Father's sermons? "But even death was powerless against the Son of God," Father continued. My assailant's hand trembled, and I braced myself for the end. "Three days after Jesus was brutally tortured and killed, he returned to life." Father's words were garbled in my ears.

With that, Pock-Marks let out a deafening roar. He flung me aside, and I collapsed onto the floor in a puddle of blood. Before I fell unconscious, I saw Pock-Marks rush toward Father, his pistol extended.

I heard a gunshot, followed by a loud thud. Darkness engulfed me, and I passed out.

PART TWO

Camp 22, Hoeryong
North Hamyong Province
North Korea

DAUGHTER OF RIGHTEOUSNESS

"May the groans of the prisoners come before you; by the strength of your arm preserve those condemned to die." Psalm 79:11

"Guess what I heard?" my friend Mee-Kyong whispered in my ear. "Officer Yeong sent his office maid away yesterday."

"Prisoners!" shouted Matron Sung, the guard in charge of our fifty-woman unit in the garment factory. When I first started working in the cutting line, I was terrified by her whip, but I quickly learned that Matron Sung was more interested in keeping her hair free from lice than she was in punishing us prisoners. Matron Sung rarely left her scent-proof box. She supervised our work from behind glass and spent her shift barking orders through a megaphone.

It was no secret that a position in the garment factory was the most lenient of all the labor jobs in Camp 22. My companions and I were still forced to work twelve-hour shifts, we were still subject to the strict 300-calorie-a-day ration, but we nevertheless felt ourselves fortunate. We were out of the Chungbong coal mine where nearly all the male prisoners were sent to work. We were spared the most abhorrent tasks, like scooping out the filth from underneath the prison toilets and carrying it to the marsh in small handle-less buckets. The fifty of us in Matron Sung's unit weren't even beaten very regularly.

Four years had passed since my mother and I first arrived at Camp 22 the morning after Father was shot. Surprisingly, Father hadn't been killed, although we were told that the bullet came dangerously near his left lung. Mother and I were sent ahead of him to a large prison camp in the rural wilderness of Hoeryong,

North Hamyong Province. Three days later, Father was transferred directly to solitary confinement in Camp 22's underground detention center.

I was also held in a solitary cell where my Father's personal guard came to torment me several times a day. "Your father, Song Hyun-Ki, must despise you," Agent Lee told me as he jammed sharp pieces of bamboo underneath my fingernails. Every day I resolved to endure, but within minutes I started screaming, begging my torturer to stop until Agent Lee sometimes laughed outright.

"You can blame your father's arrogant pride for your suffering," Agent Lee crooned as his cow-skin whip cracked open the skin of my bare back. I howled in pain which only encouraged Agent Lee even more.

After one especially brutal beating, Agent Lee took out his camera. "Now smile," he taunted. After blinding my eyes with the flash, Agent Lee studied the picture that came out of the boxy machine. "Song Hyun-Ki will be delighted to see this one. Of course, we want your father to know how well we are treating you here." With that, Agent Lee shook his head and clucked his tongue. "If only your father didn't refuse to hold on to his delusional faith. Then we could release you from detention."

Each time he came in to my cell, Agent Lee gave me an update on Father's condition. "Song Hyun-Ki was a little disoriented after his water treatment this morning," he stated with a smile. I tried to ignore his words, but I couldn't shake the image of Father suffering pathetically at the hands of such a wicked man.

And I hated Father for it.

Of course, I would be a prisoner in Camp 22 for the rest of my life; that much was never in question. Even as a twelve-year-old I knew that my future was sealed. But I also knew that there was a life outside the detention center where young children attended school, where families slept together in small huts, where in many ways life might continue on for us as it had in Hasambong.

"If only Song Hyun-Ki were not so foolish," Agent Lee goaded, "you and your parents could live together again. You could even attend classes and finish middle school. Wouldn't you like that?"

"Yes, Sir," I answered. Any future that included the chance to see the sunshine would be better than weeks locked in this underground torture chamber.

"Unfortunately for you," Agent Lee continued, "your Father needs a little more persuasion before we can release you into the main camp." And with that he forced water down my throat until I choked on my own vomit.

"Song Hyun-Ki is a traitor and a fool," Agent Lee insisted while I lay on the floor, praying for this nightmare to end soon. "If I had a daughter as bright and capable as you, I would never permit her to suffer this way. What kind of father would allow his little girl to endure such trauma just so he can hold on to his stubborn faith?"

I refused to confide in Agent Lee that these were the same questions that haunted me during my sleepless nights in my cell.

I wasn't allowed to see Mother, but Agent Lee told me that she was already adjusting to prison life as a laborer in Camp 22's furniture factory. Since Mother signed a statement denouncing any affiliation but that of the Party, the National Security Agency didn't keep her in the detention center.

Unfortunately, Father refused to sign the same statement regardless of what they did to him ... or to me. As each day brought even crueler punishment from the hands of Agent Lee, I despised my father's obstinate religion more and more. But when the screams of tortured prisoners kept me awake at night, when my entire body ached from beatings and starvation, I longed to hear Father's voice, to be in his presence, to remember the words he spoke before he was shot.

Each day I would ask Agent Lee for permission to visit Father, and each day he smiled at me. "If your Father wanted to see you," Agent Lee sneered, "he would have signed the statement of ideological conformity by now. Unfortunately, he loves his little Western god more than he loves you. It truly is a shame. I'm sure you didn't do anything to deserve such harsh treatment." After this proclamation, Agent Lee scalded my sides and my palms with fiery iron prods, now laughing at my cries, now shaking his head and proclaiming, "If only your father weren't such a fool."

Four years later, my physical wounds were healed over, leaving relatively few scars when compared to the crippled bodies of many of the older prisoners. Some individuals wasted away as forced laborers for decades; others were actually born within the confines of Camp 22's large electric fence.

My friend Mee-Kyong was one of the children who was never outside Camp 22, who was bred in captivity. We met in my eighth-grade class, which I was allowed to join after my unexpected release from the detention center. Children prisoners could attend school until they were fourteen, and I spent my first two years at Camp 22 as Mee-Kyong's classmate and friend.

Mee-Kyong's mother and father were both prisoners at Camp 22. Her mother was chosen by a National Security agent as a bride for her father to reward him for exceptional labor in the Chungbong mine. Arranged marriages between prisoners were not uncommon at Camp 22, Mee-Kyong told me. Since there was no other permissible form of physical contact between a man and a woman, marriages ordained by the National Security Agency were seen as one of a prisoner's highest possible honors. Mee-Kyong's parents were allowed to spend three nights together in a private hut, during which time Mee-

Kyong was conceived, and for the rest of their lives they lived as single prisoners in the segregated dormitories.

At least that's the story Mee-Kyong's mother told her. Mee-Kyong had a slightly more colorful version of her birth history, which she shared with me one day when our class was ordered to the outskirts of the camp to collect firewood. "A National Security agent fell in love with Mother," she whispered, all the while looking over her shoulder to make sure that our teacher wasn't watching us. Once I thought my instructor from Hasambong was strict, but that was before I met the school mistress at Camp 22.

"They had a relationship," Mee-Kyong continued, stressing the word and gauging my reaction. Of course, whatever I didn't know about intimacy after living in a one-bedroom cabin with my parents in Hasambong, I figured out pretty soon after I moved into the dorms at Camp 22.

"The guard was scared," Mee-Kyong's eyes were wide and twinkling, and she spoke about her supposed illegitimate birth as though it were the most romantic love story ever imagined. "He didn't want to get in trouble, so he picked a male prisoner at random and gave him my mother as a bride."

I watched Mee-Kyong with both envy and awe. Mee-Kyong was beautiful, with smooth skin and sparkling eyes. She even had laugh lines. I could never figure out how my friend avoided becoming vacant and lifeless as the majority of the other prisoners. She spoke of Camp 22 as if it was her home, as if there wasn't truly a free world out on the other side of the electric fence. She seemed proud of her fantasized heritage, as if the idea that her biological father might have been a National Security agent put her on a level above her peers. Mee-Kyong nodded at a guard standing in a hut on one of the watch posts that surrounded the camp. "See him?" she asked me with a wink. "Maybe he's my father."

It was Mee-Kyong's dramatic imagination and her determined spirit that helped me survive my first few years at Camp 22. When I was initially released from the detention center, Mother and I lived together in a cramped and dilapidated hut made of clay. After I told my mother about Father's fate, she and I came to an unspoken agreement to never talk about him again. Unfortunately, that silence soon became all-consuming, and within a week or so, Mother stopped communicating at all. She came home from her shift at the furniture factory, smelling of pine and cedar, and handed me my small dinner ration. A little bit later, she left again for her self-criticism session without saying anything.

At these self-criticism sessions, as I found out when I started attending them myself, the guards stood and laughed as laborers pointed fingers, blamed their peers for exaggerated sins, and made up stories of accusation against one another. These daily trials were one of the National Security Agency's many tactics to keep prisoners constantly wary of each other. Some nights the guards wouldn't release their groups until every single individual accused somebody else of wrongdoing, whether that was humming or hunting rodents or stopping to stretch in the production lines. If the guards weren't too tired, they punished the prisoners who seemed most deserving. Once the guards were finished amusing themselves, they sent everyone out. After her sessions those first few weeks of camp, Mother crawled back home and lay down on her straw mat on the floor without even looking at me.

The guards began to call Mother the "Silent One" after she stumbled and fell backward into the coal furnace one day, scalding her forearm. Even though the burn was so bad it blistered over and left red oozing welts across Mother's skin, she didn't even cry out in pain but went back to resume her soundless labor. The guards at the furniture factory found her unnatural lack of reaction so humorous that they tormented her regularly during her shift, dumping a hot coal down her back, or placing embers under her bare feet for her to stand on as she worked in the production line.

Because Mother refused to speak, even to me, I didn't know at first what was happening at the furniture factory, or why Mother came home smelling like a half-decayed corpse. Some nights she was unable to even walk, so she crawled to and from her self-criticism sessions. At first I tried to connect with her. I sat on my knees and begged her to look into my face. I knew terrible things were happening to her in the factory, but she wouldn't talk to me. Even if she had, I was so withdrawn after my time in the detainment center that I had very little comfort or encouragement to offer anyone else, no matter how closely we were related.

Soon, Mother stopped waiting in the food line for our mealtime rations. To keep us both from starving, I had to take over that responsibility in addition to my schoolwork and camp chores. It was in the queue for our meager daily meal when I first spoke with Mrs. Kan. She and I exchanged smiles or sympathetic glances on occasion, and I knew that she was one of the members of Mother's fifty-worker unit in the furniture factory. I never learned why Mrs. Kan was imprisoned with us, or how it was that she lived in one of the family units when I never saw a husband or children with her.

That night when I got to the food line, Mrs. Kan was already there, standing apart from the other prisoners and holding some small twigs that prisoners sometimes picked for firewood. As soon as I reached my place in line, she slipped in behind me. After clearing her throat, Mrs. Kan stumbled and dropped the pile of sticks. I knelt down and helped Mrs. Kan pick them up.

"Your mother is sick," Mrs. Kan whispered as we both crouched in the dirt. I looked around, wondering at first if these morbid words were indeed intended for me.

Mrs. Kan grabbed the firewood from me, and while we continued to kneel by the other prisoners in the food line, she told me in a hushed voice what the guards had been doing to Mother for the past several weeks. It shames me, beloved daughter, to tell you that instead of pitying Mother, I felt embarrassed that she would endure such torment silently. I was ashamed and angry that she didn't fight back.

"She won't live long like this," Mrs. Kan concluded.

"What should I do?" I pressed, but Mrs. Kan shook her head and stood up, wiping the dirt from her prison uniform. Perhaps Mrs. Kan already risked enough for me and my mother. If anyone saw us speaking together, Mrs. Kan would be reported at that evening's self-criticism session. Secret conversations between prisoners were forbidden almost as vehemently as sexual relations between the men and women. It was the only way the National Security agents could protect themselves against us prisoners. We outnumbered our captors fifty to one, but where there is no opportunity to communicate, there is no chance to revolt.

I returned from the food line that night, set Mother's ration before her, and tried to make her eat. Mother didn't even glance at her bowl of grains before she left for her self-criticism session. When her food remained untouched after she crawled back to our hut and went to bed, I snuck by her mat and ate her meal surreptitiously in the far corner of our cabin. The gruel made my stomach churn. I knew Mother needed the nourishment, but if she refused to eat it, should I let it go to waste when I was starving as well?

In my heart, I knew that Mrs. Kan was right. Mother hadn't touched her food in several days, and although she presented herself to her mandatory shift at the furniture factory and dragged herself to her nightly self-criticism sessions, she was already more dead than alive. The past six weeks had been so full of chaos and horror that I couldn't articulate when the last flicker of light from Mother's soul was finally snuffed out. Was it the night the soldiers burst in our cabin and carried me away, or just a few hours later when Mother denied her faith before the scar-faced interrogator? Or could it be when Mother learned about Father's final undoing once I was released from the underground detainment center at Camp 22?

The day after my conversation with Mrs. Kan, I woke up for school and couldn't make Mother get off the floor. I probably would have left her there if I hadn't been so terrified that I might also be punished for her tardiness at the factory. I pleaded with Mother and even tried to physically pull her up from her straw mat, but she wouldn't move. She stared unblinking at the wall and refused to respond to my protests. I had to go to school, so I left Mother, certain that the guards would come after her and take her away. I was living in such a primitive state of survival by then that my biggest fear was being punished for Mother's truancy. After class, I hurried home, holding my breath when I stepped into our hut. Mother was still there, in the exact position she was in when I left her. She hadn't even gotten up to relieve herself but instead urinated on the straw mat where she was lying.

I was so humiliated to see my mother in such a condition that I wanted to shake her until some spark of life or recognition lit up her void expression. I confess to you, beloved daughter, that I was more angry at Mother and scared that I might be punished for her laziness than I was hurt to see her so broken. There were no doctors I could take her to, or even a neighbor who might help. Mrs. Kan was probably the closest thing Mother had to a friend, and Mrs. Kan already took a great risk by speaking to me in the food line. I couldn't expect any further help from her. Mother was completely alone. Even I couldn't do anything for her.

The next morning I begged Mother to get up again. I screamed in frustration when she wouldn't even open her lips to drink the water I tried to drip into her mouth. But then again, like the previous day, the time came for me to leave for school, and this morning I was certain the guards wouldn't ignore Mother's absence in the factory line.

Just as I suspected, when I came home that afternoon, Mother was gone. I waited all evening in our dark hut, wondering what happened to children in the camp whose parents were too sick to work. I stayed awake most of the night, blaming myself for Mother's condition. Perhaps I shouldn't have told her the full truth about Father. Wouldn't a lie be more merciful than reality? I didn't know where Mother was, but if she survived, she would probably remain unable to work. What could be expected from a woman who refuses to eat or drink or even roll off of her makeshift bed to relieve herself?

The following morning, my teacher announced in front of my entire middle-school class, "Song Chung-Cha is the daughter of a stupid, slothful prisoner who was too lazy to get up and complete her duties for two days in a row." I was made to stand exposed in front of the class while my teacher repeatedly struck my bare bottom with a wooden plank. After this humiliation to punish me for my mother's grave misdeeds, my teacher announced, "Your mother is dead." I never learned if Mother was taken to the camp hospital to die, or if the guards somehow sped up the inevitable process. I was not surprised, nor do I remember feeling a great sense of loss. Mother had given up living a lot earlier.

From that day on, I stayed in the dorms, where girls ranging in age from eight to about nineteen all slept on the floor, head to toe, toe to head, shoulder to shoulder. Because we were only allowed to use the toilets twice a day, the dorm always smelled like urine and waste. Even though I was exhausted by the end of the day, it was hard to sleep on account of the stench. The older girls were not allowed the luxury of sanitary rags, and so their flow spilled onto the floor below us, dried on their legs, and added to the filth and squalor.

Mee-Kyong, who had lived in the dorms for a while by then, readily shared with me all of her survival secrets accumulated during her years of camp life. Always careful to ensure that nobody else was looking, Mee-Kyong demonstrated how to hunt for frogs, how to swallow a live cricket, and how to eat the meat from a raw rat. Prisoners were brutally beaten or even killed for consuming anything other than the allotted camp rations, but we would die if we didn't somehow supplement our daily handful of gruel. Many a fight broke out, even amongst us young girls, over who was the first to spot one of the scarce insects or rodents that were hunted illegally in the camp.

During my survival education as a prisoner at Camp 22, I also learned about some other ways to get by as a female prisoner. In the camp, there were favors girls could offer the guards that would ensure relative peace and comfort, including some extra food. By the time I graduated from the Camp 22 middle school, I was acutely aware of the forbidden liaisons that existed between the young female prisoners and our male captors. This overly sensual atmosphere, in spite of our squalid and primitive lifestyle, was especially noticeable in the garment factory where the prettiest girls and the most vigorous guards were sent by some unspoken rule of the camp. I was not all that surprised to find that it was the girls who were often the aggressors, practically forcing the guards to sleep with them and then demanding an extra ration of food or a blanket to cover with on the cold winter nights.

I managed until now to get through my torture under Agent Lee in the detainment center and my first two years working in the garment factory with my purity intact. But that didn't blind me to the illicit activities that went on in the guards' offices in back of the factory. I had known for a while about my friend

Mee-Kyong's association with a fiery-tempered Agent Pang. I once tried warning Mee-Kyong about him, but my unsolicited advice only made her angry. She refused to talk to me for a week. And now, as we worked side by side in the fabric-cutting line, Mee-Kyong whispered in my ear about the comrade who shared an office in the back corridor with her lover.

"Officer Yeong told Agent Pang that he wanted to find a nice young prisoner to take his old office maid's place." The role of office maid in the garment factory was a legitimate title for a few select female prisoners, but in reality the job description was hardly any different than that of a prostitute.

"You can't get involved with Officer Yeong. Agent Pang would kill you both," I added, with more seriousness than jest. I knew that if another man even walked by Mee-Kyong in the cutting line, she had to spend her entire lunch break appeasing Agent Pang's jealous wrath with every ounce of feminine charm she could muster. Even so, Mee-Kyong usually ended up with a new bruise or two after the encounter was over.

Mee-Kyong pretended to smile, but her eyes wandered to the back hallway where her lover worked. "Actually," Mee-Kyong admitted, her voice barely above a whisper, "I was thinking about recommending you."

I pretended to act surprised. "Me?" As a matter of fact, I kept trying to work up the nerve to ask Mee-Kyong to show me how to get the attention of a young guard. I was nearly seventeen years old, with no hope of ever leaving Camp 22. In the dorms I could easily point out the girls who were sleeping with the guards because their ribs didn't protrude quite as much from their sides, and their cheekbones were not quite as hollow as the rest of ours. Often they had blankets, and some wore new underclothes. One brazen prisoner even boasted of the bath she took with her lover. For those of us who were only allowed to shower twice a year, her lifestyle seemed luxurious indeed.

Unfortunately, a few weeks later she disappeared, two days after she confided in a fellow prisoner that she was pregnant.

When I thought about Mee-Kyong's proposal, however, the risks of sleeping with an officer paled next to the promise of a few extra calories. Starving to death on the meager camp rations, I didn't bother to question my conscience. I didn't wonder what Father might have said either. Father was no longer a part of my life, nor was the powerless deity he so faithfully served. It was years since I called on God's name, asked for his help, or submitted to his will.

Standing next to Mee-Kyong in the cutting line in this state of spiritual hardness, I made up my mind. My famished belly didn't allow me a hint of remorse. At sixteen, I had survived four years in Camp 22 with no one to thank other than Mee-Kyong and myself. In ten more years, if I was still alive, I would look as haggard and as ancient as the majority of the other prisoners. If I wanted to buy myself some comfort and extra privileges, now was the opportune time.

"That's a good idea, Mee-Kyong," I whispered back when I was certain the prison matron wasn't watching. "Please ask Agent Pang to recommend me to Officer Yeong as his office maid. I would be honored."

DAUGHTER OF PURITY

"Among all her lovers there is none to comfort her."
Lamentations 1:2

"Wake up!" Mee-Kyong hissed in my ear.

Disoriented and exhausted, I turned toward my friend. She held her finger over her lips and nodded toward the prisoner on night duty. As my blurry vision began to focus, I saw that the young girl who was assigned to keep watch was asleep in her chair. Prisoners in the dorm were required to serve one night shift each month. They had to stay awake and report everything that happened: which prisoners slept, which prisoners stayed awake, which prisoners complained before going to bed. They even reported sleep-talking, so every night I begged myself not to utter something incriminating while I slept.

The fact that the prisoner on night duty was asleep meant two things: that she would get a beating if another prisoner reported her, and that I could talk to Mee-Kyong about her sudden change of mood. A month ago, as if overnight, Mee-Kyong's effervescent smile gave way to a constant moody pout. I suspected Agent Pang was somehow responsible for Mee-Kyong's sullenness, but our twelve-hour shifts in the cutting line and nightly self-criticism sessions that could last for hours left little time for conversation.

"What is it?" I asked Mee-Kyong in a hush, trying not to wake up any of the other girls nearby.

Mee-Kyong rubbed her hand in a circle over her abdomen and widened her eyes.

"Pregnant?" I mouthed, trying to conceal my surprise. I never thought that Mee-Kyong might one day conceive, probably because I didn't want to admit that I might find myself

31

in the same situation one day. How could a starving teenager possibly bear a child in the squalor of our prison camp? Mee-Kyong nodded and bit her lip.

"Does he know?" I inquired, wondering what fate might befall Mee-Kyong if Agent Pang found out about her condition.

Mee-Kyong shook her head. "What should I do?" Her question surprised me. Mee-Kyong was my teacher and guide in the camp. She never asked me for advice about anything. I wanted to repay my friend for her years of kindness toward me, so I forced my foggy mind to think through Mee-Kyong's options.

She could tell Agent Pang about the pregnancy and trust that he would keep her out of trouble. Yet Agent Pang was so volatile there was no way to guess how he might react. The camp administrators generally ignored what went on at lunch breaks between the factory guards and their office maids, but Mee-Kyong explained to me that an officer who became too indiscreet in his relationship with one of the prisoners risked a shameful demotion. Agent Pang might assess the situation calmly and bribe a comrade in exchange for a pill Mee-Kyong could take, no questions asked. Or he might explode and take out his wrath on Mee-Kyong herself. I'm sure Mee-Kyong keenly remembered our fellow prisoner who vanished a year ago when she was discovered to be pregnant by a camp guard.

With Agent Pang's assistance, Mee-Kyong might receive permission from the National Security Agency to marry another prisoner. Then at least her pregnancy would appear legitimate. After a one-month maternity leave from the garment factory, Mee-Kyong could continue working with Agent Pang's baby strapped to her back. But there was no way to arrange a wedding for Mee-Kyong soon enough since prisoners were only allowed to marry on major holidays. We just celebrated the birthday of the Dear Leader's father in April, and the next possible wedding day wouldn't come until New Year's, which would be much too late into the pregnancy to protect Mee-Kyong at all. Besides, I doubted that Agent Pang would agree to let Mee-Kyong marry someone else. It was more likely that any prisoner who wed Mee-Kyong would find himself at the other end of Agent Pang's revolver before the bridal days were over.

I thought about Officer Yeong who hired me as his office maid last winter. Our relationship, though mutually beneficial, didn't involve anything of the intimacy and passion that Mee-Kyong shared with Agent Pang. I didn't dare broach the subject with him. In the four months I served as Officer Yeong's office maid, he didn't even take the time to learn my name.

Another prisoner in Mee-Kyong's situation once tried to sneak into the medical clinic to find an abortive pill but was caught and publically executed as a warning to all of the young women. I was still in middle school at the time. It had been one of my first lessons about the origins of pregnancy.

Every option I thought through seemed equally impossible. Mee-Kyong never shied away from any trial or hardship, especially if it involved the dramatic. I watched her hugging her knees and realized I couldn't help my friend. I shrugged and offered a weak smile. "I'm sorry." I hated myself for not having any advice to offer.

Instead of deflating like I expected, Mee-Kyong raised her chin. She shook her long hair and opened her mouth in a melodramatic yawn. "It'll be all right."

"What are you going to do?" I wondered.

"Do?" Mee-Kyong pretended to laugh under her breath, but ended up coughing instead. We held our breaths for several minutes to make sure none of our neighbors woke up. The prisoner on night duty remained slouched in her chair. Finally Mee-Kyong scooted closer to me. "I have time. It's not like I'll be gaining any weight the way they feed us here," she joked. "I'll make sure Agent Pang doesn't get suspicious. It'll work out."

I wanted to believe that Mee-Kyong was so resourceful she could find a way out of this dilemma, but I had seen too much in the past four years at Camp 22 to have any hope left for my friend. Even if Mee-Kyong managed to conceal her pregnancy for the entire gestation, that still didn't solve the more difficult problem.

"What will you do when the baby's born?"

Mee-Kyong shrugged her shoulders again. "I'll let you know next winter," she promised.

Playing off of Mee-Kyong's forced confidence, I smiled. Then for the first time in several years, I prayed.

As I asked God to watch over Mee-Kyong, it never occurred to me that I should be begging the Divine to protect me as well.

DAUGHTER OF TRUTH

"If an enemy were insulting me, I could endure it ... But it is you ... my companion, my close friend, with whom I once enjoyed sweet fellowship ..." Psalm 55:12-14

Through the rest of the spring and into the summer, Mee-Kyong never mentioned her pregnancy. Apparently, Agent Pang didn't suspect that Mee-Kyong carried his bastard child in her womb even as the leaves changed color and an early autumn chill settled in the camp. I didn't know how Mee-Kyong managed to keep her secret from him for so many months, but I never asked for detailed accounts of her lunch breaks in the back office.

In some way, I secretly envied Mee-Kyong and the relationship she shared with Agent Pang.

Of course, it was miserable being used by any camp officer, no matter how many extra rations you received. But at least Agent Pang cared about Mee-Kyong, even if he was violent and possessive in his passion. Because Agent Pang and my employer, Officer Yeong, worked in the same part of the factory with only a small partition separating their workspaces, I could usually hear what was happening between Mee-Kyong and her lover. They fought fairly often, Mee-Kyong daring to raise her voice and Agent Pang accusing her of falsehood and working himself into a fit until he beat her. He would then spend the next half an hour apologizing to Mee-Kyong and telling her how much he loved her. Then other times I heard sweet whispers, moans of pleasure, even laughter coming from Agent Pang's office in the back hallway.

How different were my lunch breaks spent with Officer Yeong. When Matron Sung blew her whistle, those of us girls who served as office maids in the factory went to the rooms of our respective guards, usually to the hostile stares of the other prisoners. When I entered Officer Yeong's work space, I didn't distract him from his business but applied myself quietly, fulfilling some of the basic cleaning duties that he assigned me my first day on the job.

When Officer Yeong finished whatever he was doing, he summoned me over, sometimes with nothing more than a grunt or a nod. For the rest of my lunch break, I did whatever I could to find something to occupy my thoughts, to deaden my senses, to remind myself that I was lucky to be here with Officer Yeong because, after all, I needed food to survive.

While thus engaged, I would hear the laughter of Mee-Kyong next door with Agent Pang and inwardly regret that my afternoons with Officer Yeong were the closest I had ever come to experiencing true love or romance. Unlike my naïve friend, however, I had no delusions about my employer. I knew that in a matter of weeks or months, Officer Yeong would tire of me and find his next replacement.

Mee-Kyong, on the other hand, clung to the desperate notion that somehow she and her agent would break free from their political destinies. Mee-Kyong was convinced that Agent Pang loved her as much as she loved him, and she imagined that their devotion to one another would somehow enable them to forge a future together. Her passion made Mee-Kyong so blind that she couldn't even see the high-voltage fence that surrounded Camp 22. As much as I envied my friend's idealism, as much as I fantasized about the kind of passion she and Agent Pang shared, I pitied her blind lack of reason. For her own sake, I dreaded the day when Mee-Kyong would find out once and for all what the cruel and unsympathetic world was really like.

Unfortunately, I didn't realize soon enough that Mee-Kyong's need to cling to Agent Pang would not only cost us our friendship, but jeopardize my very life.

***

On a cold September afternoon, I was in Officer Yeong's office, polishing his framed photographs of various higher-up officials from Pyongyang. Officer Yeong was an ambitious, not yet middle-aged politician, who looked toward a future in Pyongyang as a high-ranking government executive. I learned from Mee-Kyong that our respective employers were political rivals, both competing for the same position as Camp 22's Chief Officer of Productivity, an obvious catalyst into a Pyongyang career. I knew nothing of Officer Yeong's family life, though I guessed he was probably married. While Mee-Kyong's Agent Pang was charming and flirtatious, my Officer Yeong rarely displayed any emotion whatsoever. If he did have a wife, I imagined she must be bored married to a man whose only passion was for the Party and his own career advancement. Due to the nature of my relationship with Officer Yeong, however, I tried to avoid thinking about his wife at all if I could help it.

During one lunch break, Officer Yeong brooded over a thick file. The autumn rain beat against the garment factory's steel ceiling, partially drowning out the conversation between Mee-Kyong and Agent Pang in the next room. I polished Officer Yeong's portrait of the Dear Leader, wondering if I might be fortunate enough to make it through the entire lunch break without having to interact with my employer. On the other side of the partition, I heard Mee-Kyong scream.

"You filthy whore!" roared Agent Pang. I forced myself to wipe my rag across Kim Jong-Il's portrait, as if my sole purpose in life was to rid the Dear Leader's face from dust specks and fingerprints. "How long were you going to wait before telling me?" Agent Pang's voice exploded from the other side of the partition. "The whole blasted nine months?"

"It's not my fault!" Mee-Kyong cried out. I winced when I heard the sound of something crash.

"You lying dog!" Agent Pang snarled. Out of the corner of my eye, I saw Officer Yeong raise an eyebrow slightly as he studied his notes. "When did you stop taking your pills?" Mee-Kyong was crying. "When did you stop?" Until then, I didn't know Mee-Kyong was taking contraceptives. Agent Pang must have been supplying them to her surreptitiously. I couldn't hear Mee-Kyong's answer, only her sobs.

"You disgusting *prisoner*! How long have you known?"

"Two months," Mee-Kyong lied. Another thud was followed by Mee-Kyong's groan.

"You refuse to take care of things with pills?" Agent Pang questioned. "That's fine with me. There are other ways to prevent problems like this." His voice now sounded disturbingly calm. Mee-Kyong's grunts came at regular intervals. With trembling hands, I dusted the ornate frame that held yet another copy of the Dear Leader's adipose profile, but I froze immediately when Mee-Kyong mentioned me by name.

"It's prisoner Song Chung-Cha's fault." I was so startled by Mee-Kyong's words that it didn't occur to me just how scared I should be. "She's scheming with Officer Yeong. They're plotting together to make sure that he becomes the next Chief Officer of Productivity."

I didn't dare look at my employer, but I felt his body tense as he heard the lies meant to incriminate us both. I knew Mee-Kyong well enough to guess what she was doing. If she could turn Agent Pang's anger on to someone else, it would only be a matter of minutes or hours before her lover soothed the wounds that he himself inflicted, all the while proclaiming his eternal love for her.

Agent Pang was silent for a moment, and then he declared, "You're a lying whore."

"I swear it," Mee-Kyong insisted. "Chung-Cha found out about the pills. She was already pregnant by Officer Yeong, so she forced me to give them to her. She took them all so that she miscarried. I swear it's the truth. She told me that if I said anything or did anything about it, she'd report you to the Camp Director for the pills you gave me. It's all Chung-Cha's fault. She wanted to find a way to help Officer Yeong advance while discrediting you."

I felt Officer Yeong's glare heating up the back of my neck. I forced myself to continue dusting.

Mee-Kyong succeeded in averting her lover's wrath, but she still continued to spew out incriminations against me. "Prisoner Song Chung-Cha is a Christian pig." It wasn't until then that dread first hooked its talons into my spine. I had told Mee-Kyong that my father was arrested for Christian activity, but that's the most she and I ever talked about matters of faith and religion.

"She sings hymns under her breath," Mee-Kyong charged. It was a serious offense for a prisoner to hum even simple children's songs. Singing hymns was a felony, comparable to spitting on the face of the Dear Leader himself. In Hasambong, Mother wouldn't let Father teach me any religious songs for fear that I might whistle the tune in public and incriminate us all. I knew Mee-Kyong was lying to protect herself, but when the guards searched my record and discovered my parentage, the National Security Agency would have no reason to doubt Mee-Kyong's words. "Chung-Cha quotes verses to the other prisoners from that Western book of lies. She even tells her dorm mates to convert and become Christian pigs like herself."

Overcome with dizziness, I wanted to sit down but stood frozen in my place. I saw my employer reflected in the glass from one of his frames. Officer Yeong's body was rigid, his jaw clenched. My reported sins, which were about as serious as a prisoner at Camp 22 could commit, would cast a poor reflection on him as well. I was certain Officer Yeong was thinking about the Chief Officer of Productivity position, and I hated him for having used me the past eight months only to now regret the way my alleged crimes would harm his reputation.

I heard heavy boots march out of Agent Pang's room. I clenched my jaw and braced myself. Like a trapped animal I waited. The offenses my friend had just accused me of were weighty enough to land me back in the detainment center where another guard like my father's tormentor Agent Lee would break me down until I confessed to these crimes and countless others. If I were ever released back into the main camp, my body would be so broken and decrepit from my punishment that I would never find a position as an office maid again.

As much as I despised the time I spent with Officer Yeong, I regretted that I would have no other way to earn extra rations if I survived the cruel torture that I knew awaited me.

BROKEN VESSEL

"He sent forth his word and healed them; he rescued them from the grave." Psalm 107:20

As you read my words, beloved daughter, I pray that you are living in safety, with nothing to cause you excessive pain or fear. You have no need to know everything I suffered during my second stay in the underground detainment center, so I will recount only a few important details.

After Mee-Kyong's betrayal, I was taken directly to the underground chambers and locked in a small box. The sleep I managed to find was haunted with nightmares of my father's torturer, whom I never saw during my second detainment but whose menacing laugh still echoed in the concrete walls.

I was finally let out of my cage and made to sign a statement confessing to my numerous crimes: sleeping with a guard, taking stolen contraceptives, blackmailing a National Security agent, spreading religious ideology, and singing Christian hymns. I never learned what happened to my friend Mee-Kyong, whether Agent Pang paid his comrades enough yuan to keep her out of trouble or whether he rejected her, whether she gave birth to his illegitimate child or whether she simply disappeared with no God or lover or friend to rescue her. The last time I saw Mee-Kyong was when the guards dragged me out of the garment factory. Mee-Kyong, bloody and sniffling, was crumpled on the floor of Agent Pang's office. She looked up at me as the officers hauled me away. When our eyes met, Mee-Kyong let out a haunted, guttural wail that still plagues my memory to this very day.

In spite of the pain of her betrayal, I wasn't angry at Mee-Kyong. She acted out of fear and self-preservation. Mee-Kyong wasn't created to face suffering. She was too full of laughter and joy, a Korean maiden who ought to have been riding ponies in centuries past with brightly colored ribbons in her hair and a host of suitors vying for her love, instead of languishing away as a common criminal behind an electric fence. I carried around in my heart a debt of gratitude toward Mee-Kyong for the way she helped me survive as a child at Camp 22. My next four years of detainment due to Mee-Kyong's accusations – at least as I reconciled it in my own mind – repaid that debt.

Beloved daughter, there is no need to speak of the crimes that I witnessed or the hopelessness that engulfed me during those years underground. I'll just tell you that there is a God who works all things together for good. I'm convinced it was his providence which led me to the detention center, because it was there that I met the Old Woman.

Starved and battered, my body broken after years of punishment for my alleged sins, I was dying. I had been feverish for several days and was already beginning to hallucinate. Visions of eternal torture and unrest tormented me. I didn't remember enough of my father's Bible to know if I would be welcomed into a blissful paradise when I died or if a future of even greater torture and torment awaited me. I knew I should be frightened, but my body was too weak, my brain too affected by the fever to think clearly. In my delirium, I couldn't even tell if the beings walking outside my cell were real men or not. At times I imagined they were either angels or demons coming to escort me to my eternal destiny.

"What about this one?" one of the creatures said.

"She's not going to last long anyway." The voices sounded disorganized and chaotic. My eyes were closed. Rainbow-colored waves crashed and spiraled around in front of me.

"All the better. I still don't understand why the commander agreed to her request."

"You know her story. No one dares to deny the Old Woman anything." The creatures were in my cell. I opened my eyes but couldn't focus on anything. Black boots came closer and then receded until they were small specks in the distance.

"When did the prisoners in solitary confinement earn the right to request cellmates?"

The two bodies picked me up by my hands and feet. At their touch, I realized the men were made of flesh and bones. I tried to twist myself free. Did they think I was already dead? Were they there to bury me prematurely? I wanted to call out, but my mouth was parched and my throat burned.

"You know how it is with the Old Woman. Even the Commander is afraid of her."

"After what happened, I don't blame him."

They carried me down a set of stairs. I never knew there were more levels in the underground detainment center. Was this where they stored the corpses? I strained to free myself from their hold.

"She's convulsing." The guard at my arms grabbed me even more tightly.

"Looks like the Old Woman's guest might not be as good of company as she expected." The men chuckled while bright and magnificent colors spiraled in front of my eyes. I no longer felt the men at my hands and feet, nor could I sense my body swaying between them. A spiraling rainbow danced before me, lulling me into a painless, dreamless slumber.

***

The next thing I saw was a pair of blue eyes staring down at me. I blinked and sat up with ease. The burning fever that raged through my body for the past several days was gone. My throat wasn't sore or swollen anymore. I readily found my voice.

"What happened?" I asked, staring into a face full of deep wrinkles and furrows. I had never before met a Korean with such eyes.

"You are well again," sang out a deep, craggy voice. "The Lord Almighty has granted you healing." Was this an angel? I glanced around to determine if I was dead or alive. My body no longer ached, but I was confined in a small cement cell. I still wore the same oversized prison uniform I was given years ago. It was stained with blood and bile. This was certainly not heaven, but I felt healthier and stronger than I had in weeks. I couldn't be in hell either.

"Where am I?"

The Old Woman's entire face smiled. Her blue eyes twinkled. "You are in the humble cell of Myong Kyung-Soon. And I welcome you, blessed child. You are my very first guest in twenty-three years."

I stared at this ancient, blue-eyed Korean. She reached into her prison uniform and pulled out a piece of bread. I wondered if my mind was deceiving me. During my time as a prisoner, I had forgotten the taste and texture of bread entirely.

"Please eat with me, righteous daughter."

"You know my name?" I questioned.

The Old Woman studied me for a moment. "Yes, you are a righteous daughter. I am pleased to meet you, Little Chung-Cha." With that, she broke the roll of bread in two, giving me the much larger of the pieces. Then, to my utter astonishment, the Old Woman raised her eyes, lifted up a glowing face toward the cement ceiling, and prayed in a loud and fearless voice.

"Gracious Father, King of the Universe, I praise you for this bread. And I praise you for my little daughter, Chung-Cha, whom you sent here to relieve my loneliness after twenty-three years of solitary confinement. Jesus, I ask that you bless this bread for the sake of my little daughter and nourish her spirit as you have already healed her body by your power and might. Amen."

Bewildered, I glanced around for the guards I was sure would come and beat the Old Woman for her blasphemy against

44

the state. When no one arrived, I feared that I was so delirious my mind had conjured up the image of the Old Woman. But the bread she gave me was real, and as I ate, its nourishment strengthened my very soul as if by some strange power.

"My little daughter Chung-Cha has had a long and difficult journey." The Old Woman stretched out her leathery hand and tucked my hair behind my ear. My body trembled as my mind raced over the past seven years: the beatings I received from my school teacher, the humiliation I endured as Officer Yeong's office maid, the torture I experienced in the underground detainment center. In all that time, I couldn't recall anyone touching me with such gentleness.

I looked in amazement into the Old Woman's deep blue eyes, and I began to cry. I was no longer a twenty-year-old woman but a young girl of twelve, overcome with grief and heartache. The Old Woman wrapped her arms around me and stroked my lice-infected hair.

"Peace, little daughter," she whispered, leaning her chin on top of my head as she held me close to her chest. "Peace, little one. The God who heals, the Great I Am, will bring rest and comfort to your soul once again."

HEALING BALM

"I will heal their waywardness and love them freely." Hosea 14:4

"Little daughter," the Old Woman remarked one afternoon, "in the past weeks, you have told me about your friend Mee-Kyong. You have told me about the tragic events that led to your detainment here. You have told me about your mother and about the way she lost hope so many years ago. But you have not told me anything about your father. Why do you think this is?"

I sighed. In the refuge of the Old Woman's cell, I found a rest my spirit never knew before. The Old Woman taught me hymns, the songs that my Mother refused to let me hear for fear that I would end up in a place like this. I listened for hours as the Old Woman voiced her prayers of praise and thanksgiving to the God whom I forsook so long ago.

I never before met anyone like the Old Woman. While Father's faith was bold and reckless, the Old Woman's love for her Savior was peaceful and pure, as soft as the gentle spring breeze that caressed my face so many years ago. I still didn't understand why the guards allowed the Old Women to engage in such overt displays of faith. Nor could I fathom why they gave the Old Woman extra rations, why they spoke to her in hushed, almost reverent whispers, why they treated her with the deference and respect due a member of the Dear Leader's family and not a prisoner in confinement. While a guest in the Old Woman's cell, I was never hit, berated, or intimidated by a single guard. I longed to ask about the mysterious history of my hostess, but for the past two weeks, she listened only to facts about my life without offering any information about her own.

And now the Old Woman had her arm wrapped around me and was running her fingers through my hair as she did so many times. I had suffered so much at the hands of others that the Old Woman's touch was at times actually painful for me to endure. And yet I couldn't pull myself away but felt somehow cleansed and renewed, as if healing flowed from the Old Woman's very fingertips. "I think today is a good day for you to tell me about your father," the Old Woman said. There was a certainty in her voice that I couldn't argue with.

I sighed. Until the day she died, my mother and I kept our agreement to never speak of Father. I didn't even know how to talk about him anymore. Where should I start the tale? And once I started, how could I find the words to describe the end of his history?

But the Old Woman was waiting, drawing the words out of my mouth with her intense gaze.

"Father was always strong," I began, and for what must have been nearly an hour, I told the Old Woman about Father and his unwavering faith, which at one time had seemed more steadfast than the very mountains that surrounded my Hasambong hometown.

"He sounds like he was a very courageous man," the Old Woman commented after I described my father's refusal to conceal his faith when we still lived in our small cabin in North Hamyong Province.

"Yes. He was my hero," I replied. "When I was a child, I wanted to grow up to be just like him." I looked over at my cellmate to see how she would respond.

"And are you like him, righteous daughter?" probed the Old Woman. I still wasn't used to the way the Old Woman could discern my every thought.

"No," I answered, shaking my head. "When I first came to Camp 22, I was mad at Father." I told the Old Woman about my experience as a twelve-year-old in the detainment center under Agent Lee's cruel custody. "As a child I was so proud of

Father's courage and faith. But each time Agent Lee came in to beat me, I grew more and more furious at Father for not signing the statement like they demanded. And angrier at God, too," I confessed, though my doubts seemed foolish in light of the faith that radiated from the Old Woman. I looked at her to see her reaction to my words.

"The Lord remains faithful even if we are faithless," the Old Woman observed. "Little daughter, did not the apostle Peter also turn away in fear and deny his Lord?"

I nodded, remembering the story that Father taught me as a child. "Never be like Peter," Father had exhorted me. If only Father knew the future that awaited him, I thought in the Old Woman's cell, he wouldn't have made such a bold admonition.

"After ten days in underground detainment," I continued, "the National Security agent came and told me that I could start school in the main camp."

The Old Woman furrowed her eyebrows. "Why did they release you? And so suddenly?"

I couldn't stop the hot tears of shame that flowed down my cheeks. I hoped that the Old Woman would say something to fill the silence, but she was quiet.

"They let me go," I admitted and tried to take in a deep breath, "because my father signed the confession after all."

I hung my head and longed for some cleansing ointment to wash away the disgrace I felt at Father's defeat. While I was in detainment, my father's stubborn faith infuriated me. After he signed the confession, however, I had no choice but to believe that God failed him. And that thought terrified me more than all of Agent Lee's torture devices combined.

"And did they release your father then, too?" the Old Woman inquired.

"No," I whispered, desperately trying to fight away the grief that threatened to consume me. I wanted to end Father's history there, but the Old Woman continued to stare at me, and I continued to speak.

"After he signed the confession," I went on and lowered my eyes, unable to meet the Old Woman's penetrating look, "my father hanged himself in his cell."

I cried quietly into the Old Woman's shoulder until a moan of agony welled up from deep within my soul. I was powerless to control its volume. Trembling, I let the Old Woman hold me, certain that if it weren't for her strength and unshakeable faith, I would lose myself in a torrent of grief and hopelessness from which I would never recover.

The Old Woman rocked me in her firm embrace as we sat on the floor. A cautious guard approached our cell but was sent scurrying away with a flick of the Old Woman's wrist.

"He was always so strong," I lamented, unable to forget Agent Lee's horrid descriptions of my father's torture, the punishment that was so cruel and so inhumane that even my faithful father crumbled under its weight. For the next seven years, I lived in a hopeless, godless stupor. Father's suicide stripped me of any remaining faith in God's mercy or power. I was alone in a world where God was not omnipotent, where his justice and goodness did not prevail.

Yet here in the Old Woman's cell, light was able to penetrate the veil of obscurity that hung over me for so long. Miraculous healing saved me from certain death the day I was brought to the Old Woman. I still didn't know how I ended up as her cellmate, but I was convinced that if it weren't for the Old Woman's prayers on my behalf, I would have died from my illness.

Even after my health was restored, I felt God's presence again and again: in the peace and tranquility that washed over me like a soothing balm when I listened to the Old Woman's prayers, in the longing and desire that stirred in my soul when she sang her dulcet hymns, even in the incredible way we were protected from any harsh treatment from the guards. It was as if an entire legion of angels was posted at the entrance of our cell, overcoming every threat of evil in this underground chamber of torture and suffering. Heavenly mercy beckoned to me, inviting me to cleanse myself from the guilt and defilement of my hopeless, godless years as a prisoner at Camp 22.

I longed to respond to this divine love and peace that called out to my soul, to hold on to it and never let it go. But whenever I closed my eyes to pray, Agent Lee's taunting voice echoed in my mind: "Your father signed the confession this morning. He renounced his faith in God and pledged his allegiance to the Party." When I asked if I could see my father, Agent Lee's lips turned upward. "Song Hyun-Ki hanged himself less than an hour ago, a coward in death just like he was in life."

The Old Woman held me close, whispering prayers over my shaking body, as I mourned my father's defeat. Eventually, my sobbing subsided and my breathing became less spasmodic. I lay with my head against the Old Woman's shoulder, exhausted and heavy hearted. The Old Woman stroked my face, wet from tears.

"Little daughter," she declared after a long period of silence, "there is a God who works all things together for good. He takes horror and turns it into beauty. I do not know how he will redeem your pain and suffering, but I do know this: The tragedy of your father's life has some greater heavenly purpose, and the story you have just told me is far from finished."

FAMILY

"Brother will betray brother to death, and a father his child; children will rebel against their parents and have them put to death." Matthew 10:21

"Little Chung-Cha," said the Old Woman one day. The weather was getting warmer and we no longer needed the extra blankets the guards gave us at the Old Woman's request. I was regaining my strength after years of starvation and suffering. Now more than anything, I longed to breathe the fresh spring air.

The Old Woman sat with her back leaning against the cement wall of our cell. When she called my name, I stopped my anxious pacing and sat down by her side. "Have I ever told you about my family?" the Old Woman asked. It was difficult for me to hide my surprise. In the several months I had spent in the Old Woman's cell, she remained silent about her family. I didn't know what made her finally decide to talk about her past that spring day, but I was eager to listen.

"Only two of my grandparents were Korean," the Old Woman began. "When foreign missionaries first traveled to the Korean Empire, my maternal grandfather as well as my paternal grandmother both sailed over from Britain. But unlike many other missionaries, they did not just live in Korea for a few years, do good works, and then return to their lives back home. They both learned the Korean language, took Korean spouses, and died on Korean soil.

"My father was born in what is now South Korea. My mother, like you, little daughter, grew up in the mountains of North Hamyong Province. Until they found one another, Mother and Father were quite alone. It was not easy for them to be the children of Westerners, half-breeds that were never accepted by their Korean peers. They both moved to Pyongyang as young adults, my father to attend seminary and my mother to help oversee a small Christian orphanage. During the Pyongyang revival of 1906, my parents met at church and fell in love.

"At that time, marriages were still arranged by parents with the help of a matchmaker. My father and mother wanted to marry each other, so they both wrote to their parents, asking them to come to Pyongyang for a season to help them arrange the match.

"Mother and Father loved each other deeply, but for many years after marrying they had difficulty bearing children. When I was born, Father was already in his late fifties, and Mother was not much younger. By that time, the entire Korean Peninsula was annexed by Japan. Korean children were offered very limited opportunities to receive an education, so it was Mother who taught me to read and write.

"We were all still living in Pyongyang when Japan lost the Great War and the Korean Empire was divided. My parents and I tried on three separate occasions to flee to the south, but finally my parents agreed that it must be God's will for us to remain in North Korea. At that time there was still a significant Christian community in Pyongyang."

The Old Woman paused and looked at the cement ceiling above her. "Little daughter," she questioned, "do you know how many Christians live in our nation's capital today?"

At first I was sure the Old Woman was joking. *Christians in Pyongyang?* The thought was absurd. "None."

The Old Woman smiled. "Dear child, you are too quick to believe what your school instructors taught you. There are Christians in Pyongyang just as surely as there are birds outside this detainment center. These believers may be few and scattered, with very little strength or courage, but I have seen them." Perplexed, I watched the Old Woman as she continued staring up toward the ceiling. Her blue eyes sparkled, as if she were catching a glimpse of something beautiful and glorious taking place where I saw only cracked cement and spider webs.

"I have seen them." The Old Woman sighed. "My parents and I suffered much during the Peninsula War of the 1950s. We witnessed many crimes. I was twenty years old when the armistice was finally signed between North and South, and by then I was in love with an officer of the North Korea People's Army."

The Old Woman smiled, lifting her masses of wrinkles when she saw my surprise. "Like your friend Mee-Kyong," the Old Woman confessed, her craggy voice lifting with an air of youthful gaiety, "I also was once blinded by love and imagined it was enough to overcome any of our religious or ideological differences.

"My parents were heart-broken. My beloved officer was as whole heartedly atheist as they were devoutly God-fearers. They begged me not to marry him, but at this point the matchmakers were obsolete; it was the children who chose their spouses. This decorated, atheistic officer and I were married in Pyongyang, and by the time I was twenty-two, I had borne my husband two healthy boys."

I pictured my cellmate as a young mother. Traces of maternal beauty still radiated from the Old Woman's wrinkled face. I imagined her voice as it must have been decades ago, light and airy as she sang lullabies to her children at night, or doting and rich as she soothed away their scrapes and bruises with sweet words of comfort.

The Old Woman tucked a strand of my hair behind my ear and went on, "My eldest son was named Chul-Moo, a *weapon of iron*. My husband desired for him achieve a high rank in the People's Army, and from Chul-Moo's birth my husband worked in Pyongyang toward that end. When Chul-Moo's baby brother was born eleven months later, I named him Chung-Ho, as I secretly hoped that in spite of his atheistic upbringing, my son would grow up to be *righteous and godly*. I never lost my faith in Christ, you see; I just followed my heart when it came to romantic notions. Because of my parents' religious background, my husband demanded that I break all ties with them. Then, in order to protect his own military career, he bribed a comrade to change my birth certificate. If you search Pyongyang's records, you will discover that I was born to a politically auspicious family, and I have no Western blood in me."

"But your eyes!" I exclaimed, wondering how anyone could overlook those striking blue irises.

"Little daughter," the Old Woman chuckled, "if Pyongyang calls a tiger a kitten, then every single Party member will line up to pat its back and scratch that tiger's ears. In my case, Pyongyang called a half-breed, blue-eyed granddaughter of Christian missionaries a respectable Party girl. And that's exactly what I became. In spite of my husband's atheism and devotion to the Party, you see," the Old Woman continued, "I loved him, and he loved me. It was a strange three decades. I adored my husband and raised our children to be model citizens, but my secret faith made us political enemies.

"I was happier than I deserved to be. I did not have any contact with my parents, I did not know any other Christians, and I did not have a Bible. Still, my husband cherished me, my sons honored me, and I felt blessed. My only sorrow was that I could not explain the good news of Jesus to my children. And so I prayed for hours at night after my boys were asleep, pleading with the Almighty for my children's salvation. Then during the day, I played the role of an upstanding officer's wife, loving my husband and our boys zealously but never breathing a single word to anyone about my faith."

The Old Woman sighed. I was afraid she might be too tired to continue. I was glad when, after giving way to a large and noisy yawn, the Old Woman went on with her story.

"Our eldest son, Chul-Moo, entered the People's Army like my husband. He quickly advanced and even grew to outrank his father. Chung-Ho, my second-born, became a successful businessman, his work taking him into China and even the Soviet Union at times." The Old Woman smiled. "It was on a business trip to China that my youngest son Chung-Ho first heard the gospel. He immediately accepted Christ. He was afraid to tell his father, but he could not keep his secret from me. 'Mother!' he exclaimed to me the first day back from his travels. 'Let me tell you what happened to me on my trip. I learned something wonderful in China. There is a man, a perfectly righteous man named Jesus Christ. He is the Son of God. He was killed, but then he was brought back to life. He's the true and living God, Mother. And I've met him!'

"I cannot explain to you, little daughter, how my heart rejoiced at my son's confession of faith." The Old Woman beamed with the memory. "It was then, nearly three decades after his birth, that I was able to tell Chung-Ho about his true family lineage. We knew we must keep Chung-Ho's conversion from my husband, and so in many respects our lives went on as before. Nevertheless, Chung-Ho was a changed man, full of joy and the power of the Holy Spirit. When we were alone, Chung-Ho would beg me to teach him about the Bible.

"Although I praised God for Chung-Ho's salvation, I nevertheless fretted over my eldest son, Chul-Moo. He was prone to depression; he did not care for anything or anyone other than the Party and the People's Army. I suspected he was drinking heavily, although I had no proof. Rumors of an illegitimate child were threatening his career advancement. Emboldened by Chung-

Ho's conversion, I finally decided that the time had come to share the gospel with my eldest son Chul-Moo as well.

"I fasted and prayed for several days and begged my youngest son, the only other Christian I knew, to do the same. One Sunday afternoon, I went over to Chul-Moo's house as usual. 'Chul-Moo,' I told him, 'I am your mother and I love you deeply, and now you are going to sit down and listen to what I have to tell you.' And so I explained to Chul-Moo the gospel of salvation. Since I did not know how he would react to my words, I did not tell Chul-Moo that his grandparents were born of Western missionaries or that his younger brother was also a Christian.

"But Chul-Moo did not accept what I had to say. He told me that I was a Christian pig, and that even though I was his mother he was duty-bound to report me to the National Security Agency."

"Your own son turned you in?" I gasped.

The Old Woman nodded and folded her hands in her lap. "Of course, Chul-Moo knew that he himself would also be arrested if he was found to be the son of a Christian. So before he betrayed me, he spoke to a superior officer, who at that time was preparing my son for a position in the Great Leader's inner circle. Before my arrest, Chul-Moo was transferred to a detainment center along the Tumen River with new papers, a new job, and a new identity. It was a demotion, but he had done his duty to his nation while keeping himself out of prison camp."

"But how could he have done something like that to you? To his own mother?"

"Things are not always what they seem, little daughter," the Old Woman remarked. She stretched her arms and rubbed her shoulders and neck. "For years I mourned Chul-Moo's betrayal, but I wept even more for his hardness toward the good news of Christ. Still, old as I may be, I am not the Lord God Almighty; I do not pretend to know his plans for Chul-Moo, which may yet be for good."

"Were your husband and younger son arrested with you too?" I asked.

The Old Woman nodded. "After two months at Camp 22, my husband was offered release due to his impeccable record of service to the Party. The National Security Agency told him that he had to sign a statement of ideological conformity, which he did without second thought, but they also demanded that he divorce me." The Old Woman raised her chin. "Even finding out that I was his enemy did not quench my husband's love for me. He would not agree to the Agency's terms. He worked another two months in the Chongbung mine, then the National Security Agency simply announced that our marriage was annulled and resettled him in another province."

The Old Woman looked away from me. I had tried to find a way to ask the Old Woman about herself for months but always lacked the courage. Now her account did more to pique my curiosity than satiate it. Afraid that the Old Woman might grow too tired if I hesitated any longer, I cleared my throat.

"Honored Grandmother," I began, trying to choose my words carefully, "you've explained to me how you ended up as a prisoner, but you still haven't told me why they treat you so well here. Why do the guards fear you like they do? And what could you have possibly done to deserve solitary confinement for twenty-three years?"

The Old Woman sighed. "So many questions, little daughter." With a quiet grunt, the Old Woman closed her eyes and leaned her back against the cell wall. I watched her silently, waiting for her to explain more of her history. But soon the Old Woman's lips began moving in silent prayer. I finally realized with disappointment that I would have to wait even longer to find the answers to all of my questions.

CALL OF FREEDOM

"The cowering prisoners will soon be set free; they will not die in their dungeon, nor will they lack bread." Psalm 79:11

The nights grew warm. The air was humid, and I ached to feel the warmth of sunshine again.

"Summer is on its way once more," the Old Woman announced late one evening. I didn't reply; I couldn't help but think of all the summers I lost locked away in this bleak prison. Nearly four years had passed since my last breath of fresh air.

"My little daughter is quiet tonight," stated the Old Woman, who sat calmly, looking as content as if she had been lounging by a rippling brook in by-gone days.

"I just want to see the sun," I muttered. I was certain that the Old Woman would find some way to make me regret my complaints, to show me how much I had to be grateful for. In the Old Woman's cell, I was always reminded that I needed so much growth if I ever wished to be truly as righteous and godly as she.

This time, however, the Old Woman simply nodded her head. "Yes," she agreed. "It is the warmth of summer, even more so than the chill of winter, that makes me also long for freedom."

"Freedom," I mumbled, as if remembering the word for the first time. As a child, the idea of freedom brought such a melancholy emptiness. How foolish I had been to waste my childhood pining away for something other than the mountains of Hasambong. I grew up with such restlessness. And now here I was, twenty-one years old, and my only wish was to see the blue sky or the green grass again, even if for a moment.

The Old Woman studied me as I brooded. After several minutes, she moved over beside me and held my gaze with her steady blue eyes. "Our souls' yearnings remind us that heaven is our true home," she remarked. "It is only there that we will ever find real and lasting freedom."

Her words were far from comforting. "Does God expect me to wait until I die here before I see color again?" I asked. "Or feel the wind? Or gaze at the stars?" I looked at the Old Woman's pale complexion and immediately despised myself.

"I'm sorry. I shouldn't complain. Not to you." The Old Woman began her solitary confinement in this cell before I was born, yet she had such a peaceful contentedness about her that I never wondered before if she also pined away for fresh air, for sunlight, for freedom.

The Old Woman clucked her tongue. "You have no reason to apologize," she assured me. "Little daughter, the reason that you are restless for freedom is that God has plans for you that extend beyond the walls of this prison." The Old Woman squinted as she studied me. "As for me, I know that I will die in this cell." She raised her hand to silence my protests. "That is my fate, and my assurance of it is God's gift to me. But you, righteous daughter, you have the seal of freedom upon your forehead. The Lord will not forsake you behind these prison walls. Your destiny reaches beyond the borders of this camp." As I listened to the Old Woman's words, something swelled in my heart that I hadn't experienced in my entire detainment:

Hope.

"The Lord will lift you up on angels' wings," the Old Woman proclaimed, breathing faith and conviction into my languishing soul. A sense of power and truth tarried in our cell, so poignant that I held my breath to keep from spoiling its beauty. "God Almighty will himself provide you safe escort beyond prison walls, over rivers, even across borders of nations." I stared at the Old Woman, not daring to move for fear of destroying the spell of life and inspiration that her words cast upon my troubled heart.

Then suddenly, without warning or reason, the Old Woman chuckled. The sound startled me. "Little daughter, why do you keep on gazing at me as if I were something supernatural?"

"Your words," I stammered. "What you just said ..."

The Old Woman smiled. "Without a doubt, the Almighty reveals his thoughts to me, but that does not make me any less human than you yourself are."

I shook my head. "You're so much stronger than I could ever hope to be. You have a boldness I've never seen before." *Except in my father*, I might have added, were it not for his recantation and suicide in the detention center.

"Dear child," she chuckled, "do you truly think that your old cellmate is really a bold witness for Christ?"

Now I was even more puzzled. "But aren't you?" The Old Woman stopped laughing and shook her head.

"No," she confessed. "At least I was not always." The Old Woman smoothed out her gray hair. "Have I told you about my youngest son, Chung-Ho?"

"You told me of that he was converted in China, and that he was arrested with you and your husband."

"There is more to that story." The Old Woman shifted her weight. "When my son Chung-Ho was brought to Camp 22, the Lord placed upon him a spirit of great boldness and courage. By the time Chung-Ho was taken to glory, he had already shared the gospel with dozens, maybe hundreds, of prisoners. Many perishing souls were saved because of Chung-Ho's fearless witness."

"What happened to him?" I asked, although I was already certain of the answer.

"He was killed by the National Security Agency." The Old Woman cleared her throat. Her head drooped toward the cement floor where we sat side by side, our shoulders and knees touching. I had never before noticed how frail her bones were. "It was a public execution. Because I was his mother, and because I was a Christian, I was forced to stand in the front row, so close that my prison garment was stained with my son's blood."

I turned to study the Old Woman's ancient face, trying for a moment to understand her pain and sorrow. "But even those standing half a kilometer away would have heard his voice that day," the Old Woman related, once again lifting her head up. "Even though he was bound and tied to the execution pole, my son managed to release his gag, then preached the gospel to every single prisoner and guard who was blessed enough to witness his execution.

"'Fellow prisoners,' he called out, 'This is the day of my death. Today I experience true freedom for the first time.' Before the guards pulled their triggers, my son urged everyone listening to call on the name of Jesus and receive eternal life."

The Old Woman sighed and patted my hand. "Chung-Ho's faith and courage shamed me. As an officer's wife, I never shared the gospel with anybody besides my two sons, and even that took me years of prayer and fasting. The day Chung-Ho was shot, I begged God to give me my son's boldness. But the Almighty did not answer my prayers overnight."

"Then how did you end up here?"

"That is a different story altogether," answered the Old Woman, coughing before she continued in her low, melodic voice. "Eventually word of my witnessing attempts, feeble as they were, reached the ears of the guards. I was put in detainment. It was then, in the midst of intense fear and persecution, that the words of our Master came to me in a vision. One night, the Savior himself appeared in my cell and told me clearly, 'Do not be afraid of those who kill the body but cannot kill the soul.'"

"From Matthew," I remarked, remembering how my father loved the first gospel and memorized it in its entirety. The Old Woman looked over at me and furrowed her brow.

"Matthew?" she repeated. "From the Bible?"

Now I was confused. "Isn't that where that verse is from?"

The Old Woman smiled. "Little daughter, your father was blessed to have the Word of God not only in his heart, but in his hands, and you were blessed to have him as your teacher. I have not seen the Holy Book since I was younger than you, a child in my parents' house before the Peninsula War. As an adult, I never owned a Bible out of fear of my husband." I tried to picture my cellmate afraid of anything, but the image would not come to me.

"My vision of Jesus filled me with hope," the Old Woman continued. "It was then that the Lord revealed to me that I would die a prisoner here in the detainment center, so I stopped fearing the torture of men and began to proclaim the gospel of Christ. The guards and prisoners probably all thought I was crazy. I sat alone in my cell, hollering loudly so that everyone within hearing range would have a chance to receive salvation. To my surprise, I did not die within a few days or weeks as I expected. The Lord sustained me through the beatings I endured, so I continued to preach. Eventually the National Security agents put me down here in solitary confinement where my voice would not carry so far."

The Old Woman lay down on the ground. The lights were already off for the night. Refusing to let her sleep before answering my final question, I clasped her bony hand. "But why do the guards treat you the way they do? There isn't a prisoner in the entire camp as well off as you!"

The Old Woman didn't roll over. "Little daughter," she sighed, "I am very tired, and I must be getting some rest now."

"But can't you just explain ..." I pleaded, but the Old Woman's mouth drooped open. She was already asleep.

VISITOR

"And all who touched him were healed." Matthew 14:36

"Honored Grandmother," a male voice whispered. I quickly awoke, startled to see the shadowy form of a guard hovering over the Old Woman. Few of the guards came down our corridor at night, and none ever entered our cell before. His flashlight was covered almost entirely with a rag, and his whisper was strained as he shook the Old Woman. "Honored Grandmother."

The Old Woman's joints groaned as she sat up. After turning to face the guard, she stretched out her arms and smiled at him broadly. "Comrade, welcome to the home of Myong Kyung-Soon and my little daughter Song Chung-Cha. We are honored by your visit."

The guard shifted uneasily at the Old Woman's greeting. "Please, Honored Grandmother," he whispered, looking down the hallway, "it is my daughter." The guard paused and rubbed his pants leg. "She is very ill."

"And you have come to ask me to pray for her healing," the Old Woman finished.

"If you please, Honored Grandmother," begged the guard. "I've heard about the night so many years ago, about what happened to you. I wouldn't dare to ask you for help except that I have no one else. My wife is dead. My daughter is all I have left."

The Old Woman stared at the man, who continued rubbing his arm up and down his leg as he endured her silent scrutiny.

After a moment staring at our guest, the Old Woman lifted her head toward the ceiling. She sat in silent meditation while the guard cast furtive glances down the hallway.

Finally, the Old Woman opened her eyes and looked directly at our visitor. "You may go now," she announced. "But remember that it is Jesus Christ, and not Myong Kyung-Soon, who has healed your daughter."

The guard stood up and bowed awkwardly. "I am indebted to you for your kindness, Honored Grandmother." He rushed out of our cell and locked the door behind him.

"May the Almighty protect you both," the Old Woman whispered, but by then the guard was running down the hallway. In a moment, he was out of sight.

I watched the Old Woman and tried to guess what it was that made the guards not only fear her but also solicit her prayers for the miraculous.

As the Old Woman lay herself back down on the cement floor, her body creaked in revolt. "Little daughter," she called out softly in the darkness, "are you awake?"

"Yes, Honored Grandmother," I answered, inching myself to her side, ready to ask her my questions.

"Dear child," she rasped, squeezing my hand weakly in hers. The Old Woman coughed. "I am very tired. Would you do me a favor?"

"Anything," I promised, as curious as I was earnest. I wondered what I could possibly do to repay the Old Woman for her friendship and encouragement.

The Old Woman took a deep and labored breath. Inside her chest was a dry rattle that made me cringe. "Such a dear child," she croaked, almost to herself. It was not until that moment that I realized the Old Woman's body was subject to sickness and weakness just as mine was. The thought was terrifying. "I am so very tired," she repeated. "It would be an honor if my little daughter would pray over my weary soul and body."

I confess to you, beloved daughter, that I was disappointed by the Old Woman's request. I was ready to strip off my clothes in order to give my friend extra warmth, to forgo food for a week in order to provide her with additional rations, to deny myself sleep in order to offer her my lap as a pillow as she did so often for me.

Nevertheless, I couldn't refuse the Old Woman's request, however incompetent I felt. I held her feeble hand, shut my eyes, and mumbled some pitiful prayer about comfort and rest and protection. I was certain that I failed the Old Woman, but when I was done, she pressed my hand weakly and whispered, "Thank you, little daughter" before another coughing fit racked her entire body.

HOVERING

"We ourselves ... groan inwardly as we wait eagerly for our adoption as sons, the redemption of our bodies." Romans 8:23

The next day I was surprised to find the Old Woman still asleep when the electricity was turned on. Every morning for the past nine months, I woke up to the sound of the Old Woman singing hymns or speaking her prayers in her low, croaking voice. When she saw me, she would stop and smile, the joy from her face illuminating our entire cell. "And how is my righteous daughter today?" she would ask. We would spend the rest of the day together in quiet rest or deep conversation.

But this morning, the Old Woman didn't wake up as usual. Her breathing remained as rattled as it was the night before. Through her threadbare prison garments, the Old Woman's ribcage pulled and tugged with each labored breath. I didn't want to admit to myself what was clear before my eyes: my friend and mentor was sick. A familiar sense of fear and dread swept over me. I still couldn't understand why I was here in this cell, but I knew that my nine-month respite from beatings and torture was solely the result of my relationship with the Old Woman. My body grew hot and ached with memories of torment and agony.

As I watched the Old Woman sleeping, looking fifteen years older and ten kilograms lighter than she did the previous day, an even deeper fear than that of torture crept into my spirit. In the Old Woman's presence, I experienced peace and joy like I hadn't known since before Father was arrested. If the Old Woman died, I was terrified that every ounce of conviction that was born once again in my heart after my father's death would be buried with her forever.

God, I prayed, *I need her so much. Don't take her away.*

The Old Woman moaned and cracked open one of her blue eyes. "Little daughter?" she whispered. I rushed to kneel by her side. I touched her forehead. The Old Woman felt cold and moist.

I squeezed the Old Woman's hand; her presence seemed to be my only source of hope or strength. "What do you need?" The Old Woman looked at me and squinted without answering. I tried to slow my racing heart and then asked again, "Can I get something for you?"

"Water," the Old Woman croaked. Her gray hair hung over her forehead in clumps.

I ran to the locked door of our cell. "Help!" I called out through the bars. "Please help us!" Although I never addressed a guard in my entire tenure in the detention center, I didn't worry for my safety. I knew the guards scurried like ants to show the Old Woman their deference and wasn't surprised when two prison officers came running down the hallway.

"What is it?" the senior guard demanded.

"She's sick," I replied. "She needs water." The first guard nodded his head slightly, sending his younger comrade scurrying down the corridor.

"How long has she been like this?" the guard demanded, clasping the bar to our cell door. His forearm muscles bulged underneath his uniform.

"She said she was tired last night," I related, "and she was like this when she woke up this morning."

The younger guard returned and unlocked the cell door to hand me a small tin cup full of water. I carried it over and sat down on the floor next to the Old Woman. I propped her head up on my lap and held the cup as she sipped at it. Water dribbled down her chin onto my leg.

"Thank you." The Old Woman sighed as I felt her moist forehead again.

I looked toward the guards, who continued to hover by the door. "I think she went back to sleep," I reported.

"Then that is all we can do for now," said the senior guard. "We will keep water here for you to give her. If she needs anything else, you must let us know."

An hour later, I was trying to pray when I heard the Old Woman. "My son," she spoke. The words were slurred. Her eyes were still closed. "My son," the Old Woman repeated, her body rocking slowly from side to side. "How does a good tree bear such fruit?"

"Grandmother?" I whispered.

"The sheep wears wolf clothes," the Old Woman mumbled. Drool dripped from the corner of her mouth. "My son ... a black sheep ... not a wolf ..."

I forced myself to sit by her side, but it sent tremors through my backbone to see the Old Woman, who had been a constant pillar of strength and refuge, reduced to such a delirious state.

The Old Woman muttered incoherently for several hours. Eventually, a third guard appeared and handed me an extra blanket and mug of hot tea. I took the gifts in terrified silence. My only friend was hovering at the threshold of death.

There would be no miracle worker to save her.

PART THREE

North Hamyong Province
North Korea

FURNACE

"We went through fire and water, but you brought us to a place of abundance." Psalm 66:12

"Hurry up, filthy prisoners!" the guard shouted at us. The Old Woman had been dead for eight months. Two months after her death I was released unexpectedly from underground detainment, but my eyes still stung in bright lights. The agent's whip flicked against the back of my prison uniform and grazed my skin. The young girl at my side grabbed my arm.

"I can't go in there!" She cried out as the flames lurched toward us. She was only a teenager, no older than I was when I first went to work in the garment factory. The guard's whip snapped through the air a second time and landed on the girl's back. She fell to her knees with a sob.

"Stand up," I urged, dragging the prisoner by her elbow. Together, we shielded our faces with our arms and entered the blazing building.

"We're going to die!" the girl yelled.

"No," I assured her, "we'll be fine. That guard's not coming in here. He won't hurt you anymore." As I stared at the leaping flames before us, I knew that it wasn't the guard the girl was afraid of.

"Hurry!" I called to her, shouting in order to be heard over the roaring blaze. Dozens of prisoners from the garment factory were dispatched with us to put out the flames in the train depot by Camp 22's Chungbong mine. Eventually, the guards realized it was hopeless to save the building, so they ordered those of us still alive to enter the burning station to salvage the most important documents. I held the young girl's arm and looked around for the metal file cabinets that contained the bills of sale, shipping orders, and production records that were more valuable to the National Security Agency than the lives of us prisoners.

The smoke burned my lungs, but I couldn't gasp in enough air to force a cough. Above the howls of the inferno, I heard a loud crackling. A smoldering beam fell from the ceiling, nearly striking my companion's head.

"We're going to die in here!" The girl shrieked and dropped to the floor. I turned and knelt down to help her when another prisoner grabbed me from behind.

"There's no time!" he shouted. "Move!" He jerked me up by my arm and pulled me forward just as the roof collapsed behind me. I turned around and saw a pile of debris, almost as tall as myself, right in the spot where the girl had been kneeling.

"Are you hurt?" questioned the man who saved me. I shook my head. There were no other prisoners in sight. "My name is Shin," he said. "You better follow me." The main entrance was completely blocked off by rubble so we crawled farther in. I longed for fresh air, wincing in pain with each short breath of soot and ash.

This was my first time in the train depot. Shin and I eventually made our way to a semi-enclosed tunnel. A current of fresh air howled through, and I coughed so hard that I vomited bile.

When my body stopped convulsing, I looked around and saw a single train track. Ladders and empty crates cluttered the wooden platform where we were lying. "What is this place?" I whispered, resulting in a second coughing fit. I hunched over as my lungs tried to clear out the black soot from the fire.

Shin made his way over to the far side of the station where long shadows hid a pile of crates in almost total obscurity. He turned several empty boxes on their sides and made a small enclosure against a corner of the building. As he worked, Shin beckoned me to come closer. Still too weary to stand, I crawled over and joined him behind the crates.

"What are you doing?"

Shin put his finger to his lips. "They won't finish sorting through all this rubble for days. If we disappear on the morning train, wouldn't they simply assume we were dead?"

My heart raced. "You can't really be thinking of escape," I hissed before another choking episode seized my body.

Shin patted my back in a feeble attempt to quiet my coughing. "I can't stay here," he explained. "I have a daughter. I need to find her."

"They'll send you to the detention centers if you get caught," I warned Shin. "Do you have any idea what they'd do to you there?"

Shin cringed. "I know more about it than you could guess."

I looked away. What right did this prisoner have to assume that he, or anyone else, had witnessed more heinous crimes than I in those underground torture cells?

I would have voiced my argument but froze when I heard footsteps. Shin pulled me behind the crates, and we both ducked down behind them.

"No one here," shouted a man.

"Check around," another voiced sounded from farther back. "Make sure nobody's hiding by those boxes." I held my breath, tried to swallow away another cough, and willed the shadows and darkness to cover us both. Our shelter of crates now seemed a shamefully inadequate refuge. Visions of torture back in the underground detainment center ran unchecked through my mind.

The guard approached our makeshift tower. I could glimpse portions of his olive-green uniform through the slats of the crates. He stuck out his toe and gave our structure a half-hearted kick when a gunshot sounded from nearby. Shin and I both jumped, and I'm certain that I gasped aloud, but the guard was already running back toward the smoldering building.

"Catch her!" a voice from within the depot shouted. "Prisoner, stop!"

Someone else called out, "She's heading for the tracks."

Two more gunshots rang out, followed by a warbled cry and a thud just a few meters away. I squeezed my eyes shut and begged my lungs to breathe evenly. For a moment there was silence, and then I heard boots approaching the end of the plank. I bit my lip to stifle another cough.

"Is she dead?" a man asked.

"I would say so," answered the second.

"Should we clean it up?"

"Leave her there. The train will arrive in the morning. It should make her a pretty example for anyone else thinking of escape."

Still trembling, I listened to the guards' receding footsteps. I sat in a terrified daze for what must have been at least an hour, but nobody returned.

Eventually, the full moon began its nocturnal ascent. The hoot of an owl interrupted the stillness, and for the first time I realized how cold it was.

"You're shivering," whispered Shin. I didn't say anything. Thoughts of freedom and escape intermingled with the dread of discovery and detainment. "Please," Shin continued, shifting his weight, "let me give you my coat." Before I could react, Shin wrapped a makeshift burlap jacket around my shoulders. His hand brushed against my cheek, and he cleared his throat.

I thought about Shin's words: *"They won't finish sorting through all this rubble for days. If we disappear on the morning train, wouldn't they simply assume we were dead?"*

Would they? It sounded more like wishful thinking than trustworthy logic to me. But if I went back to my unit at camp, wouldn't the guards punish me? Wouldn't they assume I tried to help the prisoner whose body now lay within a few meters of my handmade refuge? I thought about faking an injury from the fire, but the inner building was already searched. Who would believe me?

Fear kept me crouched behind the crates. I didn't want to escape with Shin. I knew it would never work. But I couldn't forget the Old Woman's words that continued to beckon to me eight months after her death: *"You have the seal of freedom upon your forehead."* The Old Woman had been so convinced that I would one day throw off my prisoner uniform and escape the confines of Camp 22. *"God Almighty will himself provide you safe escort beyond prison walls."* In spite of the Old Woman's confidence, my fear of punishment was just as strong a restraint as Camp 22's electric fence.

I wasn't willing to flee, but I knew it was too late to return to the dorm. The self-criticism sessions were probably halfway done by now. And so I waited.

Wishing I were safe with my unit, I begged the darkness to conceal me and the dawn to arrive quickly.

LIGHT OF DAWN

"The path of the righteous is like the first gleam of dawn, shining ever brighter till the full light of day." Proverbs 4:18

There are some sounds that are so sweet, so sacred in the recesses of my mind, they will always remain with me: my father's confession in the Hasambong precinct building, the Old Woman's hymns of praise, the train's whistle as Shin and I escaped Camp 22 crouched hidden in a coal car.

For the first time since I was a young girl of twelve, I was outside the heavily patrolled borders of the camp. Yet as I hid in the train car that raced me away from my prison of nine years, I knew the road ahead of me held many dangers.

It was just before dawn, and there was not enough light in the coal car to allow me to study my fellow runaway. I thought about our conversation last night, when Shin and I sat side by side behind our makeshift shelter of crates in the train station. Shin spoke briefly of his young daughter. He arranged safe passage into Yanji, China for her eight months earlier.

"My wife is dead," Shin explained in the darkness. "My little girl is all I have left."

Based on his appearance and speech, I tried to guess Shin's age. He was skinny but not yet emaciated; in spite of his internment at Camp 22, he still appeared to have most of his health and vigor. I wondered about his past, but Shin remained elusive. I suspected he was well-off, both financially and politically, before his arrest. I figured that sending a minor to China safely required significant bribe money and appropriate contacts. Shin's burlap coat revealed a resourceful survival instinct. Although he didn't become a prisoner until sometime after his daughter's escape, Shin seemed familiar with the train depot's inner workings. When the train arrived hours before sunrise that morning, Shin knew the precise time that we could emerge from our hiding place, when both the conductor and the guards were preoccupied. Right before we slipped into one of the coal cars, Shin opened the door easily in spite of its complicated locking system.

Because Shin was risking detainment, torture, even execution at the hands of the National Security Agency in order to be reunited with his daughter, it was obvious that he was a brave and devoted father. Yet how he coordinated his escape with a fire in the train depot, how he became so familiar with the minute details of train depot procedures after only a few months of imprisonment, or why he chose to put himself in even more danger by inviting me to flee Camp 22 with him, I could only wonder.

Shin told me that the train ride to the Kimchaek steel mill would take about three hours. I was exhausted, but even once we were relatively safe in one of the coal cars heading away from Camp 22, I still couldn't sleep. Shin and I sat side by side behind large crates of coal, with no room to stretch our legs. My neck and shoulders ached.

"You should rest," Shin advised. "Once we arrive in Kimchaek it's a long journey to the Chinese border."

Although my body was exhausted, my mind raced as fast as our train to freedom. Yesterday, I woke up in the dorm with my unit, hoping to complete my twelve-hour shift at the garment factory with minimal discomfort. Now here I was, still wearing my prisoner's clothes, preparing to follow a stranger all the way from Kimchaek to the northernmost region of North Hamyong, where we would try to cross the Tumen River into China.

"You can't sleep, can you?" Shin finally asked.

"My mind won't slow down," I confessed.

"When I was a boy traveling to the coast with my family," Shin began, confirming my suspicions that he came from a wealthy heritage, "my father would tell us stories. Perhaps you could tell us one to help the time pass more pleasantly."

"I don't know many stories." I wished that my childhood included opportunities to learn the tales that a respectable lady might tell her traveling companion.

Shin cleared his throat. "You do know one story." From where I sat, I tried to make out Shin's face in the early light of dawn.

"Song Chung-Cha," Shin implored, although I never told him my family name, "will you tell me who Jesus Christ is, and how it was that eight months ago my daughter was healed by his power?"

HAUNTED

"To what can I liken you, that I may comfort you, O Virgin Daughter of Zion? Your wound is as deep as the sea. Who can heal you?" Lamentations 2:13

For some time, the only sound was the loud droning of the train's engine and the protest of its heavy wheels over the tracks. Finally, I found my voice.

"That was you?" I squeaked, remembering the Old Woman's nervous visitor the night before she died.

Shin nodded. His face, still covered in soot from the train depot fire, was now visible in the dim morning light. He took my hand in his. I recoiled from his touch.

"When did you become a prisoner?"

Shin lowered his gaze. "I never was a prisoner." He spoke to the floor.

I stared at the detention guard, trying to understand his words. Little by little, what was at first enshrouded in mystery became clear: Shin's relative health and strength, his familiarity with the mining depot, his knowledge of the train schedule.

"And the fire?" I didn't mean for my voice to quiver as much as it did.

"I needed a distraction if we were to escape," Shin admitted. "It was for my daughter."

My empty stomach churned. "But those people …" I thought about the young girl whose body was probably still buried underneath a pile of burnt rubble.

Shin stared at me. I was shocked that he could raise his eyes to meet mine. He didn't flinch or blanch. My body grew rigid in fear as I understood exactly who Shin was and at what price he bought our freedom.

"How could you?" I felt dizzy. Even though I was sitting, I reached out and held onto a crate of coal to steady myself.

"You don't have a child," Shin explained. Perhaps if I met Shin three years later, I would have understood his words. But that day, when the idea of having a daughter of my own to love and protect was as distant as the Chinese border itself, I found no sympathy to offer this blood-stained detention guard.

"You sacrificed dozens of innocent lives just so you could escape!" I protested.

Shin winced and swallowed so hard I could hear his throat working. "Please understand." He reached his hand out toward me.

I slapped Shin away and tried to push my body as far from him as possible. "Don't touch me!"

"Please," Shin implored. "It wasn't me. I wasn't there that day. I had no part of it." The fact that Shin even knew the reason for my violent reaction only increased my panic. I began trembling as memories of bodies – so many bodies, all of them sweaty and filthy and defiling – reached out from my past and grabbed hold of me once again.

"I wasn't there," Shin insisted. "I was at home that day with my little girl."

I knew what Shin was trying to do. He was trying to tell me that he wasn't really one of *them*, that although he wore the officer's uniform, he didn't belong to that group of beasts in the detention center who mocked God, heaven, and everything holy the day the Old Woman died. Shin wasn't the kind of officer who would defile a corpse just hours after death, tempting the Almighty to avenge himself on all of humankind right then. While Shin's comrades swarmed and tormented me, Shin was at home, thanking an unknown deity for his daughter's miraculous healing.

Trapped with Shin in the speeding coal car, I never felt so abandoned: by the Old Woman whose unexpected death left me alone and defenseless at the hands of boorish beasts, and by God who took her away and did nothing as I was mistreated in the same cell where I once found such refuge. I even felt betrayed by Shin, the man I imagined was my deliverer but who turned out to be no different than those creatures who abused me the day the Old Woman died.

I feared I might either kill Shin or die of panic before we ever reached Kimchaek. Shin's hands that were trying to comfort and calm me were no different than the hands of the many officers who misused me one after another following the Old Woman's death. I tried to push him away, scratching at his face, no longer able to separate the present from that morning eight months ago.

***

When the Old Woman died, a stagnant dread fell upon the entire detention center. Everyone, including myself, waited in silence for some supernatural display of power and vengeance. The Old Woman's body was left untouched, and officers gathered around the door to our cell in rapt attention. I wondered if an earthquake would split the ground to swallow them alive or if lightning and heavenly fire might find its way to the bottom floor of the concrete structure.

Atheist guards, suddenly superstitious, did whatever they could to appease the Old Woman's God. Many agents laid offerings outside our cell: rations of bread and grain, a cup of tea, even some dried meat. A few of the men called on the name of Jesus Christ, not knowing who or what he was, but apparently hoping that if they showed him enough reverence he would refrain from unleashing his fury and wrath upon us all.

I sat and waited, wondering if the Old Woman's prophesy regarding my freedom was about to be fulfilled. I wouldn't have been surprised to see my father's friend Moses, the legendary hero of my childhood, come marching down the stairs to escort me to my safe haven in front of dozens of National Security officers.

Instead ... silence. An hour passed. I kept watching, expecting to see some semblance of life or beauty in the Old Woman's body that her spirit so recently abandoned. There was only the stillness and finality of death. The Old Woman's mouth hung open with an empty, almost senile, gaze. Her eyes, which I expected to be shining with joy at her long-awaited homecoming, were cross, and her brow was furrowed.

After a few hours, the guards grew tired of their fearful and reverent wake. One or two began to chuckle, making jokes and mimicking the Old Woman's imbecilic, open-mouthed expression. I sucked in my breath when one of the men unlocked the door to our cell. While a few guards lingered in the hallway, most entered and stood around the corpse, some laughing, some cursing the memory of my friend.

I sat in the corner, hoping to stay unnoticed. A bottle of soju was passed around, and the soldiers increased their jocular irreverence. The fear of the Old Woman, which held every single one of her guards captive for as long as I knew her, was suddenly lifted. The mood turned celebratory.

"Here's to you, old hag!" exclaimed a guard, splashing his repugnant liquor on the Old Woman's face and chest. While I huddled in the corner, begging the shadows to conceal me, the Old Woman's body and memory were defiled in every way imaginable. Then all too quickly, her abusers turned on me.

"Here's the witch's little pupil," exclaimed one guard who was already slurring his words.

"Perhaps the Old Woman taught her how to cast a spell on us."

"She can put a hex on me. I don't mind."

"Come here, girl-witch. Let's see if the Old Woman or her God have any power left to protect you."

***

I shielded my face and shrieked, unaware that I was in a coal car next to Shin and not back in the Old Woman's cell at the merciless treatment of godless creatures.

"Please! Stop screaming." Shin begged. "Someone might hear you. We could be caught. *Please!*"

I opened my eyes and saw Shin, bloody claw-marks etched across his sooty cheeks. "You're safe now," Shin promised. "It's just me."

Shin didn't touch me as I whimpered softly into my palms. My teeth chattered in rhythm with the train's lurching.

"I had no part in what those guards did to you that day." I hated Shin for his pitiful attempts to comfort me. How did he expect me to react when I found out what he was? With joyful gratitude? I might have accused him to his face, but instead I wanted even more to forget that he was in the coal car beside me, as if by my sheer will power I could make him disappear and free myself from these haunting memories.

"You need to rest." I didn't want to acknowledge Shin's presence by arguing with him. At least asleep, I could try to forget he was there. A moment later I was unconscious, while dreamless slumber offered only partial relief from the ghosts of my past.

JOURNEY

"I lift up my eyes to the hills – where does my help come from?"
Psalm 121:1

"Wake up," a man whispered, shaking me out of my fitful and troubled sleep. I blinked in confusion, wondering why my shirt was soaked with sweat and why my body was rushing through space.

"Hurry," the man urged. "We don't have much time."

I was not awake enough to remember why I was crouched beside crates of coal. My mind felt foggy, and my body still trembled slightly from some trauma I couldn't recall. The man opened the door to the train car, letting in a blast of salty air. I had never been to the coast before. The smell startled me awake.

"We have to jump," Shin explained above the roaring of the train. He reached out for my hand, and when I took it I recoiled at his touch as if by some latent instinct. Suddenly remembering who this man was, I looked around for any other means of escape. The detainment guard looked at me with wide eyes. "It's the only way. Please, come with me."

There was no choice. I could feel the train slowing down on the tracks, and I needed to be out of the car before we reached the steel mill. As much as I loathed Shin, I decided that being trapped with a detention guard was still better than being sent back to prison camp and punished for my escape. I held my breath and watched the ground racing by beneath my feet.

"Jump!" Shin shouted. Still holding my arm, he leapt off the platform. I hesitated a moment too long so that it was the weight of Shin's body being jerked downward that yanked me out of the coal car, causing us both to roll and land dangerously close to the tracks.

A sharp rock broke my fall, knocking the air out of me. For a horrifying moment, my lungs were paralyzed and I couldn't breathe at all. Shin approached to help me up, but I waved him away with a determined hand and forced myself to stand up on my own.

"How do you feel?" Shin cleared his throat and stared down at my feet.

I shrugged away his question. The last thing I wanted was to speak to this detention guard about my waking nightmare on the train. "Fine," I declared through gritted teeth.

Shin shifted his weight back and forth. "We'll need more food." Shin eyed me up and down, standing several paces from me with his hands hanging limp and useless by his side. He had taken off his prisoner clothes in the coal car and now wore a drab civilian's shirt and khaki pants. I still had Shin's burlap coat over my gray uniform. Shin didn't speak of my outburst on the train but only commented, "You look too conspicuous. You'll have to stay here while I buy us some food."

Shin helped me hide as best as I could in the outskirts of the city limits by what appeared to be some abandoned sheds. He promised to come back to me within an hour, and I waited in tortured uncertainty, wondering if it would be better to flee from Shin and his unforgiveable and dangerous past or to continue on with him to China.

I knew that there was no way for me to survive if I tried to stay there in Kimchaek. I had no papers, no trade, no relatives. I didn't even have regular clothes. For a moment I contemplated abandoning Shin and trying to find my way to the Chinese border by myself, but thoughts of the Hamyong mountain range to the north kept my feet planted firmly on Kimchaek soil.

When he returned, Shin handed me a winter coat and lined snow boots. "Where did you find these?" I asked, unwilling to accept stolen goods as a gift from this National Security agent.

Because I had been in Camp 22 since the worst of the famine, I didn't know about the ten-day markets, nor could I have guessed that Shin planned our escape to coincide with a market day in Kimchaek where he could legally purchase food and supplies for the upcoming mountain trek.

Shin didn't say anything. He shook his head and helped me cover my prison uniform with my new coat, taking painful efforts to keep from touching me directly. His delicate, almost fearful, treatment was humiliating. I grumbled a coarse "Thank you" as Shin handed me my shoes. I pulled them on awkwardly. They were the first boots I ever wore.

After Shin packed our new supply of food in the burlap bag that once served as my jacket, we walked northwest toward the interior of North Hamyong Province. Shin walked a pace or two ahead of me, every now and then glancing back and asking how I was doing. I refused to answer. Shin was in much better physical health than I. Even if I wanted to talk to my companion, the uneven terrain would have made any discussion difficult. It took all my focus to keep up with Shin's pace without stumbling.

Shin and I stopped right before nightfall in a thick forest grove that sheltered us from the wind and the worst of the cold. We shared a small roll and ate a few roots, careful to ration our food to last for as much of our journey as possible. We were still a two-day's hike from the mountains themselves, and once we arrived at their base we would spend at least another week crossing their wintery passes.

It was too dangerous to light a fire this close to town, so we sat with our backs to the wind and shivered with cold. It was Shin who first tried to break the strained silence.

"You are a courageous girl." Shin stared at a tree branch where a solitary brown leaf flapped in the howling wind.

"You can't think me courageous after this morning." I

poked the snow with a small stick while the defiant leaf flapped in the breeze.

"I know how brutal guards can be," Shin whispered into the night. I winced at this unwelcome reminder of exactly how familiar Shin was with the torture and cruelty of the underground detainment center. I wrapped my arms around my chest and turned away from him. "But you have your spirit left." Shin reached his arm out to me and then dropped it to his side again. "You carry around in your heart a hope that is a mystery to me."

I shook my head. "You must be mistaking me for the Old Woman."

Shin packed a handful of snow into a ball and threw it at the leaf, which finally surrendered and fluttered into the snow bank below. "You just don't know how strong you are," he grumbled.

WEARY TRAVELER

"For my yoke is easy and my burden is light." Matthew 11:30

Shin and I woke up the next day with the sunrise. We skipped our morning meal and continued walking northwest. I was so unaccustomed to wearing boots that in the afternoon my feet erupted in painful blisters.

"I'm afraid we can't stop yet," Shin apologized. We were too close to the inhabited area of Kilchu-up for comfort, he explained, and we still had several more hours to walk before we could stop safely to build a fire. By nightfall, the soles of my feet were covered with open sores.

When we finally found a forested area to spend the night, Shin cut long strips off the top of his burlap bag and bandaged my wounds with gentle hands.

"I'm sorry." I didn't even think to ask what he was apologizing to me for.

The following evening, after yet another day of hiking in strained silence, Shin bandaged my blistered feet again. Shin cared for my wounds with such tenderness that I might have expected him to be a life-saving physician instead of a detainment center guard who worked for the National Security Agency. It was that night I finally found my voice.

"How old is your daughter?" I asked. The treetops were covered in hoarfrost that reflected the grayish-pink of dusk.

"She is seven," Shin told me. I was surprised, expecting her to be older. While he dressed my second foot, Shin told me of his family. "My wife died of complications after childbirth. Our daughter was born with club feet ... and some other abnormalities." Shin glided my boot on, careful to disturb the bandages as little as possible. "Since the doctors believed our daughter's condition might be genetic, my wife was sterilized. She died of infection when our daughter was only two weeks old."

"And you raised her by yourself?" I asked, trying to imagine how a man whose job was to torture and kill could nurture his own child when he went home from his shift at the detainment center.

"She went to nursery school, allowing me to continue my work at the ..." Shin stopped himself. "Allowing me to stay employed." He rubbed his hands together before putting his gloves back on. "There never was a sweeter child born. When she turned five, they didn't let her attend grade school. She couldn't talk. She wasn't even toilet trained and had many other problems." I wondered if the guards Shin worked with knew about his daughter's disabilities. A tender father who doted on his handicapped kid didn't seem to fit the image of the typical National Security agent.

"Her grandmother, my mother-in-law, moved in with us to care for my little girl while I was at work," Shin explained. For a brief moment, I considered the possibility that all of the detainment center guards I met over the years had children of their own. The idea was incomprehensible.

"Why did you send her to Yanji?" I asked, trying to think of something else.

Shin wiped his brow with the back of his hand. "Because of you."

"Me?"

"Last summer, my daughter developed an infection in her lungs and couldn't breathe properly. The doctors refused to give her medicine. They said she didn't deserve medical care." Shin turned his head aside and spat in the snow.

"I was desperate. After my wife died, my daughter was the only light in my life. I knew the Old Woman's story. So I asked her for help. I'm sure you remember that night. When I returned home, my mother-in-law was awake. She told me how my daughter's breathing cleared up in an instant, at the same time I was in your cell.

"When I got to work two days later, I learned about what happened to the Old Woman. And what happened to you as well." I stared at the snowy carpet beneath me while Shin continued. "Any hope that I had left in the Party vanished. We weren't victorious upholders of the revolution; we were barbarians. Gruesome, cruel beasts. My colleagues and I were not even fit to be called humans.

"But I was scared," Shin confessed. "I knew what would happen if I openly rebelled. So I sent my daughter on to Yanji for her own protection and made a vow to the Old Woman's God that I would do everything in my power to correct the mistakes of my past and make up for the shameful behavior of my comrades.

"I used my position in the detainment center to help as many as I could. A few, like yourself, I sent back to the main camp. But my authority was limited, and eventually my colleagues realized I lost my zeal to their cause. I was demoted. They sent me to guard the train depot. It was a lesson meant to teach me not to interfere with camp politics.

"With my daughter no longer by my side, I grew very depressed and withdrawn. If you must know, I came close to drastic measures." Shin paused and lowered his head. "Suicide," he finally admitted.

I cringed at this confession, not because I felt sorry for Shin and the anguish of his past, but because I couldn't shake the image of my father hanging in his cell after denying the God he once loved so passionately.

"What stopped you?" I asked, trying to rid myself of the horrific picture.

"You did," Shin answered. "I knew that you were close to the Old Woman. If anyone could explain her mystery to me, it was you."

I sighed. "Then I am destined to disappoint you. She spoke very little about herself during our entire nine months together. There's not much I can share with you." I regretted that I didn't press the Old Woman harder to tell me the rest of her story. In the comfort of her cell, I imagined that she and I would always enjoy unhurried days filled with easy conversation and restful silence. I never realized that my respite with the Old Woman would be curtailed so abruptly.

"I'm not talking about the Old Woman's past," Shin commented, "although it was undoubtedly miraculous. I'm talking about what happened the night I was in your cell. The Old Woman told me that it was Jesus Christ who healed my daughter. I've heard this name before, but I don't know who this man is or whether he is dead or alive. And I don't understand how my daughter was healed on his account. That," Shin concluded, "is what I wanted to ask you for eight months. That is why I decided to take you with me when I escaped to Yanji."

For the first time during our conversation, I turned and stared at Shin. "You planned to escape with me from the beginning?"

Shin nodded. "I knew what unit of the garment factory you were working in. It wasn't difficult. When the fire started I gave orders for the women from the garment factory to come put it out."

"But you were wearing prison clothes when you found me," I recalled.

"I acted like I had to find some important papers. The fire had already claimed several lives by then; it wasn't hard finding a uniform." Shin pointed to his civilian shirt and pants. "I wore these under my guard clothes that day. I planned it all several weeks in advance, you see."

I shut my eyes. My feet stung from the blisters as well as the cold. "I did what I had to do," Shin insisted. "My hands were already stained with the blood of innocent men, women ... even children." I didn't want to hear such a confession and tried to silence Shin with the shake of my head. He wouldn't stop. "I need to correct my past. For eight months, I've done what I can to appease your God, but I still have no rest. No matter how much good I've done, I'm still haunted by my guilt. Can't you help me, you who were so close to the Old Woman and her Lord?"

I stared at Shin who finished bandaging my feet and was pacing restlessly back and forth in the snow. "What must I do to finally experience the peace my soul needs?"

"I wish I could tell you," I answered. But even if I knew the answer myself, I wondered if I would share it with this blood-stained detainment guard.

MOUNTAIN CLEFT

"His way is in the whirlwind and the storm, and clouds are the dust of his feet." Nahum 1:3

As we continued on our journey through the wintery mountain passes, I grew more comfortable with Shin's company. Shin told me of his childhood as the eldest son of an important Party cadre. I told him of Father and his bold and relentless faith.

"If I was there," Shin proclaimed after I told him of Father's death, "I would have ripped out Agent Lee's throat with my bare hands." I was dependent on Shin for my very survival, but I remained terrified of his violent outbursts. I never forgot that it was men like Shin who destroyed my father, who defiled the Old Woman's body, who abused me so severely in the underground detention center. I longed to believe Shin when he told me of his repentance eight months earlier, but I couldn't forget that my freedom from Camp 22 was purchased with the lives of innocent prisoners. In this way, my savior was also my captor, enslaving me to himself by my fear of his ruthless past.

Shin often asked me about my faith, but my answers were never enough to satisfy him. Shin wanted to experience the power, the peace, the love that he had seen in the life of the Old Woman. Alone with Shin in the middle of the Hamyong mountains, I realized that I didn't have the spiritual bread to satiate his soul's deep hunger.

"Do you believe all your tales of Jesus?" Shin questioned one evening as we sat huddled by a blazing fire. A snow storm forced us to seek shelter in the opening of a small mountain cave.

"Of course," I declared, wondering how much snow would fall before we could resume our journey. At Shin's insistence, I shared with him again the stories I remembered of Jesus' life, his crucifixion, and his resurrection.

"But what does it *mean?*" Shin demanded while the snow piled outside, covering the trail behind us. It was still early in the evening, but storm clouds completely concealed the sun. Our only light came from the small fire in our cave opening.

"I suppose," I stammered, "it means that since Jesus died, we can go to heaven and have eternal life with him there."

"Couldn't God have granted mankind eternal life without crucifying his only Son?" asked Shin. "I wouldn't give my daughter up for anything. How could any parent, even the divine, make such a sacrifice?"

"I don't know." I tried to think of how my father would have responded to Shin and his incessant questions.

"And if Jesus was God," Shin wondered aloud, "then why wasn't his resurrection enough to erase evil from this world entirely?" The stormy wind howled at our backs and hurled bursts of snow into our refuge. I shivered from cold and wrapped my coat tight around me.

These were mysteries of theology that I never wrestled with. God was either a part of my life, or he wasn't. During my times of faith, growing up in Hasambong and then living under the Old Woman's tutelage, I simply believed what I heard. But Shin needed more than Bible stories and platitudes. He was searching for that peace that he found in the presence of the Old Woman. His soul thirsted for spiritual drink, but I didn't know how to lead him to it. You can see at this point in my life, beloved daughter, my own spirit was still quite parched and dry.

"The Old Woman once told me," I began as we stared into the diminishing flames, "that God uses the evil in this world to fulfill his own purposes."

"But why?"

I groped for the words that would make me sound intelligent and reasonable. "Perhaps God wanted us all to choose our own destinies, be they for good or evil." My response seemed as weak as the fading fire.

"But without divine intervention," Shin countered, "every single one of us would choose the evil."

I wished for something to say to show Shin that I was his equal, that I could help him find the answers that he so desperately needed. "God's wisdom is not like the wisdom of this world," I offered, but my own words sounded so uncertain. I knew it was a dismal response to address the deep doubts that plagued Shin's soul. "At least, that's what the Old Woman said." I thought about my deceased friend. How I regretted not having more time with her. "I wish she were here."

The dying embers reflected in Shin's eyes. "I have never yet met a more powerful woman." It's hard to explain to you why my heart ached at these words.

We were both quiet for a moment, our backs wet from the snow. Finally Shin muttered, "I wonder why God didn't kill those guards the day she died." Shin threw a twig into the remaining flames. "I would have."

I shuddered, as I often did when Shin spoke so morbidly. "Did you know the Old Woman never owned a Bible?" I asked, hoping to distract Shin from his menacing thoughts. "The last time she even saw one, she was younger than I."

"She didn't need a Bible," Shin mumbled into the smoke. "She had the truth stamped upon her heart." I sensed another one of his black moods coming over Shin, and I wanted to pull him out of his self-focused misery.

"Perhaps once we get to Yanji, we can find a Bible and study it together," I offered, then grew embarrassed by the suggestion.

"*If* we make it to Yanji," Shin grumbled. For a moment, I thought about telling Shin about Moses, the man who smuggled

Father's Bible from China, but I stopped myself. Shin's connections to the National Security Agency were too recently severed, his past too violent. I couldn't betray the trust of another, especially one so powerful and indispensable to the underground Korean church as Moses.

"Do you know what was most remarkable about the Old Woman?" I began again, in one last attempt to lighten Shin's soul by my trite conversation. "She seemed to know the future. It was the Old Woman who told me that I would escape the camp." Shin looked up for a moment, then threw another twig in the fire.

"She was always talking about me, or listening to me talk about myself," I remarked, remembering the sound of the Old Woman's throaty voice. "During all those months when we were together, the Old Woman never even had the chance to tell me why the guards were so afraid of her."

Shin looked straight at me. Perhaps my confession was enough to jerk Shin out of his melancholy, at least for the present. "She didn't?" My words weren't quite true; the Old Woman had plenty of opportunities to tell me of her enigmatic past, but she chose not to for some unknown reason.

"For over a year I've felt like I've been left out of a great mystery," I admitted.

"It truly is a mystery," Shin agreed. I was thankful for his renewed interest in our conversation. Shin shifted his weight and swept some snow off his shoulders. "The Old Woman's son was killed by the guards."

"She told me about that."

"Yes, but did she tell you what happened in the camp on the day of his execution?"

"She said that her son began preaching to the crowds, urging them to convert."

"That was before they shot him," Shin stated. "Within minutes of his death, while he was still bound to the execution pole, the sky covered over with clouds. They say the day was completely clear, but in a matter of minutes it was pouring down rain." If the Old Woman's son were killed in the summer, there would be very little unusual about a sudden rain storm. I waited for Shin to continue.

"That very hour, lightning struck the administration building and nearly burned it to the ground." As I listened to Shin, I was mesmerized by the growing firelight reflected in his dark eyes. "The guards were afraid, thinking it must be some kind of an omen. Then they forgot about the storm and the fire. Until the following summer."

"What happened then?"

"The Old Woman was in the detainment center," Shin recounted, "but she refused to stop talking about her Jesus. So eventually the guards decided to kill her. They didn't want her to start proselytizing like her son had at his execution, so they took her secretly to a gallows that used to stand by the officers' quarters.

"Guards at the camp are always trying to come up with unusual ways to execute prisoners," Shin stated. I felt myself again withdraw in fear from Shin and his brutal past. "They say that the Old Woman was placed in the noose and made to stand on her toes until she eventually collapsed and hanged herself. She stood there for two and a half days," Shin proclaimed, his eyes wide. "She never wavered, never fell asleep. Knowing her, she was probably singing hymns the entire time." I grinned when I remembered the Old Woman's love for sacred music.

"One officer told me they took bets to guess when the Old Woman would die. No one expected her to survive a third night, so several guards stood watch, for recreation more than anything else." I wondered how anyone could speak of an execution so casually.

"There was another fierce rain storm that night," Shin went on. "Then, just like her son did, the Old Woman started preaching to those guards gathered around to witness her death. She proclaimed the name of Jesus well into the night, but eventually her voice grew too tired to continue. The guards could see that she was beyond the point of human exhaustion. She was soaked by rain and hadn't slept in nearly three days.

"The Old Woman's eyes finally started to close. Everybody there was certain she was about to collapse and hang herself, when a bolt of lightning struck the noose and broke it. The Old Woman fell to the ground, and when one of the guards finally worked up the courage to check on her, she was quite alive."

In spite of everything I knew about my friend, it was hard to believe that such a peculiar set of events really happened.

"From that time on," Shin added, "the Old Woman was placed in solitary confinement. The guards were instructed not to harm her in any way. People were afraid that her death would bring great judgment upon the entire camp." I thought back to the fearful looks of the officers the morning the Old Woman grew ill, and the offerings of appeasement laid at the door to our cell after she died.

"What's even stranger," Shin concluded, "is that when the guards went back to look at her records, they found out that lightning delivered the Old Woman from death on the exact anniversary of her son's execution."

I didn't bother to ask Shin how much, if any, of the Old Woman's story was embellished over the decades as it was passed down from one officer to another. I was thankful for his conversation, thankful that I managed once again to keep Shin from succumbing to the dark depression that I feared might one day consume him entirely.

We talked about the Old Woman for a little while longer and then stretched out on the floor of the cave. My heart was heavier than usual as I thought about my former cellmate. When I knew her, the Old Woman's life was surrounded by such secrecy. Now that I knew all of her tale – however miraculous – that mystery was stolen away from me forever.

I wrapped my coat around my chest and tried to fall asleep. Instead I lay still listening to the howling wind as it whipped through the entrance of our small mountain cave.

UNMERITED

"For it is by grace we have been saved." Ephesians 2:8

Three weeks after the fire in the train depot, Shin and I arrived in Hasambong. The harsh weather and my poor physical condition had kept us from crossing the mountains as quickly as Shin planned. We ran out of food after reaching the mountain peak and subsisted on bark and whatever roots we could dig out of the snow.

I wish I could explain to you, beloved daughter, exactly how I felt when my hometown came into view. Nine years had passed since the inspection unit stole my parents and me away from Hasambong. I was only a child then. In those nine years away from home I suffered unspeakably, but I survived.

We were too conspicuous to pass through Hasambong directly, and so we sat on a small hillside overlooking my hometown. We waited for nightfall, hidden in a thick forest of the pine and fir trees that stood out so starkly in memories from my childhood.

"My old grade school is over there," I told Shin, pointing to the weather-worn building near the Tumen River. "And there's the precinct building." Nine years ago, as I was dragged away to prison camp, I never expected to see that place again. "That's where my father was shot."

"I've been wondering," Shin commented as I stared at so many familiar landmarks, "what was it your father said the night he was arrested that made the guards so furious?"

I thought about that night at the precinct building often, but my memories weren't of the words uttered but of the terror I felt before wickedness and evil triumphed once and for all. I stared at the precinct building, trying to remember what Father said so many years ago. "He was bold. He was willing to risk his own life, and even mine, for his Savior."

"Why?" Shin pressed. How could I explain to Shin what I didn't fully grasp?

I tried to imagine how Father would answer Shin's question. "Well," I started, "Father loved God even more than he loved his own life."

"But to put his child at risk!" Shin exclaimed. I was certain Shin was thinking of his daughter on the other side of the border. "How could a loving father do something like that?"

In my past I despised Father for what he put me through, but I wasn't willing to listen to Shin voice such doubts himself. "My father loved me more than you could ever imagine."

Shin opened his mouth but then closed it again. I stared at the precinct building in silence. "I still don't understand," Shin confessed after a few minutes. "Surely God wouldn't punish your father for trying to save you. Would he?"

I bit my lip, wishing Shin would ask me about something else, anything else about my hometown. "Father's faith didn't really work that way," I told him. "I don't think he worried much about God punishing him." Shin leaned toward me. "Father loved Jesus. He obeyed God because his heart overflowed with thankfulness, not because he was trying to escape punishment or win the Lord's approval."

Shin rubbed his hands together. "He didn't try to earn God's favor?" I shook my head. Shin leapt up and began to pace in the snow.

"Because no mortal could ever earn the favor of the Almighty," Shin went on. I was shocked when Shin's eyes met mine; for the first time since I met him, Shin's face was shining with joy. "It's not about what we can do for God. We can't do anything good on our own." Shin spoke rapidly now as he voiced his thoughts out loud. "It's not a matter of just trying harder. It's a matter of love and simple trust." I longed to be caught up in Shin's newfound discovery, but instead I was baffled. Shin may as well have been speaking to me in the language of the Chinese patrol guards whose watchtowers stood fixed across the frozen Tumen River.

Shin grabbed my hand. I wondered how a simple philosophy could bring Shin so much happiness. "That's what the good news is," Shin proclaimed. "It means that we can never offer God a life of true obedience. Instead it's his power and love that make us acceptable to him."

I was glad for Shin's apparent epiphany, but my mind was still stuck in the precinct building nine years ago, my ears still ringing with the echoes of gunfire.

THE CROSSING

"Whoever hears my words and believes him who sent me has eternal life and will not be condemned; he has crossed over from death to life." John 5:24

Shin and I lay down to rest in the dense forest overlooking Hasambong. I don't think I've ever missed my father as much as I did that night underneath the starry sky. Even sleep didn't ease the hollow ache in my heart.

Shin shook me awake in the middle of the night.

"It's time," he announced to the starlit stillness. We had already decided that tonight was the night we would sneak across the Tumen border into China.

I rushed with Shin toward the frozen river, praying that the border patrolmen wouldn't see us. We arrived at the bank of the Tumen a little while later, panting hard and sweating in spite of the cold.

"Only think," I whispered, hoping my forced confidence might bring us good luck, "you'll see your daughter soon."

Shin stared off into the distance. "Before we go, I need to tell you something." He turned to stare at me with fierce intensity. I flushed in spite of the cold night air and for some reason wondered if he was about to kiss me. A dog howled in the distance, jerking Shin into action. His thoughts still unspoken, Shin held my elbow, and we ran as fast as we dared on top of the ice and snow, crouching in the starlight. As soon as we started moving, I regretted not waiting for a cloudy night. With all of my senses heightened, the air was animated with noises: a twig breaking, Shin breathing heavily by my side. When we reached the middle of the river, the ice groaned loudly.

"It's about to crack!" My body tensed and refused to move.

Shin grabbed my arm. "That ice is at least half a meter thick," he assured me. "You're as safe as you were on the shore. Now, hurry." If Shin weren't by my side, I would never have found the courage to continue across the frozen river. As it was, Shin pulled me along so that even if I wanted to turn back, I wouldn't have been able to break free from his hold.

Shin and I made it to the opposite bank and fell in the snow. We paused by a small grove of bushes. I was no longer on Korean soil. Any sense of joy or exhilaration at our successful river crossing, however, was quickly dispelled when I heard a dog snarling. When I was a girl, I watched the Chinese guards patrolling the border with their wolf-like canines. I never imagined having to confront one of those beasts face to face.

Shin put his finger to his lip, and with his other hand he grabbed my elbow. We listened again; the canine's warning growls were coming closer. Immediately Shin stood up and pulled me, half running, half tripping, up the riverbank.

In an instant, white lights from a watchtower illuminated the night sky. "Faster!" Shin called out. My lungs were bursting with exertion and fear. I begged God to protect us. A rock jutting out from a snow pile caught my boot. I screamed as I fell to the ground. My face slammed into the snow.

Shin was already several paces ahead, but he turned back and ran toward me. "Get up!" he shouted as another round of machine-gun fire sounded from the opposite direction. Shin gasped and fell on top of me. I tried to push him off, but he wouldn't move.

"Stand up!" I begged. I reached to wipe some melted snow off my face. It was hot. And it wasn't snow.

Was I shot? I explored my bloody face with my fingers. The blood wasn't mine. It was Shin's. I felt my friend's neck for a pulse.

He was dead.

Closing my eyes, I finally managed to roll Shin off me. I ran ahead, leaving Shin's body there at the edge of the riverbank.

I didn't stop. Nearly blinded by tears and fright, I ran for what felt like hours until I collapsed. I crawled on my belly underneath some bushes with briars that tore at my coat and scratched my face. As I wiped Shin's blood on the snowy dirt beneath me, I was confronted with the horrifying truth that I was alone, an illegal immigrant in a foreign country. I had no family. I had no friends.

And now, I didn't even have anyone to guide or protect me.

PART FOUR

Sanhe
Jilin Province
China

WORDS WITHOUT KNOWLEDGE

"My ears had heard of you but now my eyes have seen you.
Therefore I despise myself and repent in dust and ashes."
Job 42:5-6

I didn't know the name of the city I was hiding in. I had no idea which road would take me to Yanji. And what would I do there if I managed to find it? Shin was dead. The winter coat he purchased for me back in Kimchaek was stained with his blood, and my ears still rang with the sound of machine guns. The moon was low on the horizon. It wasn't dawn yet, but I guessed sunrise was only a few hours away. Whatever plan I was about to conceive, I needed to come up with it soon.

I was too scared, or else I would have fled back to North Hamyong Province that very night. Although my terror of guard dogs and watchtowers kept me on the Chinese side of the border, I didn't know where to go or what to do next. To travel to Yanji in search of some disabled seven-year-old didn't make any sense. Even if Shin's daughter was alive and I was somehow able to trace her whereabouts, I would only endanger the child as well as her caregiver by contacting them.

The starlit sky looked just like it did when I gazed up at it as a young child in my Hasambong home, only now I was completely alone, a refugee lost in a country that didn't want me and wouldn't shelter me.

And why didn't God let me die instead of Shin? So that I could perish alone and forsaken in a foreign land? Why did Shin turn around to help me? Shin's training as a detention guard should have taught him to leave me as easy prey for the guard dogs. Wouldn't it be better if I perished and Shin lived?

Then Shin could have gone on to find his daughter. Whom did I have in China? Whom did I have in the whole world? *Why did you bring me here?* I demanded of God, who seemed to be mocking me by my mere survival. Any idealistic dreams I once held about China being a land of promise and freedom were dashed. Shin was dead. Although I didn't yet know about the significant bribes the Chinese police offered for refugees, I did know they would send me back to North Korea if they found me. If Shin hadn't helped me escape Camp 22 in the first place, I would be asleep now in the dorms. In an hour or two I would wake up to another shift in the fabric-cutting line. I wouldn't have blood stained on my coat and on my face. I would know when my next meal would be, even if it was only a few bites. *Why did you ever let me flee?* I asked under my breath. *It would have been better for me to die than to live.*

I pray, beloved daughter, that you have never felt so abandoned, so hopeless that you have dared utter such blasphemous words. But as I hid myself, stained in Shin's blood, I poured out my heated complaints before the Lord. I demanded that God give me an account for my father's cruel and painful death, for my mother's slow and silent one, for the Old Woman's desecrated memory, for Shin's decision to help me escape Camp 22 only to perish and leave me stranded in a foreign country.

I wish that I could tell you how God spoke soothing and comforting words into my soul as I hid trapped under a thorn bush. But he did not.

Nor was he silent.

The Almighty responded to my complaints. And when he did, I was horrified at my outburst and my appalling lack of faith.

The stars shone above, each one proclaiming that the Creator I accused of injustice and wrongdoing was infinitely more powerful than I could ever fathom. The cold wind stung my face, reminding me that the God I charged with negligence was to be feared more than any National Security agent, armed border patrolman, or ravenous watchdog. The thorns of my hiding place broke open my skin. I had no choice but to admit that my misery didn't compare to the punishment I earned by my own rebellion against God. In spite of my life's nearly unbearable trials, I was still experiencing more grace than I deserved.

That night, I saw myself as I never had before. I was not Song Chung-Cha, Hyun-Ki's righteous daughter who was occasionally forced by circumstances to go against God's commands. I was Song Chung-Cha, who never once lived up to my name, who had no righteousness or piety at all to offer the Almighty to atone for my grave offenses of bitterness, doubt, and faithlessness.

I accused God of sin when he allowed my father to perish. I assumed that a holy God would excuse my adulterous relationship as Agent Yeong's office maid because I was doing what I had to do to survive. I denied God's omnipotence when he didn't intervene while I was mistreated by over a dozen guards in the Old Woman's cell. I spent years at Camp 22 living in either passive or open rebellion, refusing to bend my knee to the God that failed to prevent my family's arrest so many years earlier.

I was horrified at my own shortcomings. To spend a lifetime in the detainment center seemed a far more bearable sentence than to fall into the eternal judgment of the God I had spurned repeatedly over the past twenty-one years.

Have mercy! my tormented soul pleaded. I remembered what Shin told me just hours before his death: *"No mortal could ever earn the favor of the Almighty. We can't do anything good on our own."*

Have mercy! my wounded spirit cried out into the terrifying darkness. My sinfulness and rebellion were so obvious to me now.

Have mercy! I begged again to the just and righteous Judge of both the living and the dead. It wasn't until that moment, when I was almost certain that the earth would swallow me whole and deliver me directly to the gates of hell, that I felt God's loving touch.

Beloved daughter, I wish I could be telling you this story face to face. You might read my words and imagine that the Almighty isn't compassionate toward us, or that he doesn't understand the pain and wounds of our hearts. The Almighty does see our brokenness, and he reaches out to us with indescribable grace and love. It's just that I couldn't accept his mercy and forgiveness until I first repented of my own rebellion against him.

Only seconds after my own guilt silenced my profane charges against the Almighty, I was surrounded by warmth. Even the air I breathed felt sacred. I couldn't see anybody, but I was certain that Jesus himself was in the thorn bush with me, holding my head on his lap, pouring his grace into my war-torn soul, healing my spirit's deep wounds with the gentle touch of his nail-scarred hands.

The questions that had plagued my soul for years remained unanswered, yet where there was previously turmoil and unrest, there was now peace and the unshakable certainty that God is both loving and powerful. Even though men are brutal, sinful from birth and unable to do any good, even though innocent children, worrisome mothers, and courageous fathers each suffer every day in God's created world, I knew in my heart that God is still good. And somehow, in the core of my spirit, I was certain that I was loved and cherished more than I dared imagine.

The wind howled, and the night sounds mourned the darkness that had covered the entire earth since sin first entered the world. I was a stranger in a foreign land, hungry and disheveled, but in my soul there was light and rejoicing.

I was a child of God. I was his righteous daughter. And I was loved more than I had ever dreamed possible.

HAVEN

"They were glad when it grew calm, and he guided them to their desired haven." Psalm 107:30

I didn't intend to fall asleep. I was startled to see the sun above me when I woke up the next day. I was still lying underneath the thorn bush and could hardly move. The asthmatic sting in my lungs reminded me that I had been running yesterday. How far? I knew that something devastating happened, but my groggy mind refused to wake up as fast as I pleaded it to.

I looked around as far as I could from my hiding place and saw nothing familiar. All too slowly, I recalled fragments of the previous evening: machine guns in the night, blood on my cheek, a prayer whispered in hiding.

And then I remembered everything.

My breathing sped up. My throat constricted. Begging myself to remain calm, I thought through my options. I could turn myself in to the North Koreans, but that would only mean torture and a future back in prison. I couldn't return to Hasambong and live secretly there. I had been imprisoned in the camps since my childhood and didn't know how to survive on my own. But what was I supposed to do in China to avoid getting caught? I didn't know anything about Chinese geography; I didn't even know what province I was in.

At first, it seemed that my only choice was to return to my own country and surrender myself to the Korean guards. Perhaps after their interrogations, they would let me live out the rest of my days in a labor camp like the one I left only three weeks earlier. If I claimed that Shin kidnapped me, I might get a lighter sentence than other border crossers.

Then I remembered the godlessness and hopelessness of my years at Camp 22. Was my faith strong enough to sustain me through that much suffering again? Spending the rest of my life in the same bleak spiritual stupor was a fate worse than death itself.

I must confess to you, beloved daughter, that if I had a weapon with me that day I would have been tempted to end my life right there in the thorny copse. I was terrified of the road ahead of me, certain that it could only lead to more heartache, more suffering, and more trials to test my fragile faith. If God let me down even one more time, I would never have the courage or spiritual stamina to trust him again. I was too scarred by my past and too terrified of my future to realize that God's hand could guide me there on Chinese soil.

Because I was in such an emotional state, perhaps you will not be surprised when I tell you that it was nearly evening when I finally crawled out from under the thorns. My heart was weighed down with so much fear and uncertainty that I spent another hour or two crouched between two bushes, cringing in fear at the slightest sound. Other than a pair of sparrows, the area was deserted. I wondered just how far I ran last night. The watchtowers and the riverbank were now out of sight.

Somewhere in the recesses of my memory, the Old Woman's words played over again in my ears: *"The Lord will lift you up on angels' wings. God Almighty will himself provide you safe escort beyond prison walls, over rivers, even across borders of nations."* Yet with the Old Woman's prophecy of hope came so many doubts about God's goodness and power like those that tormented me ever since Father's death. How can a powerful God watch idly while his children suffer? If God was able to keep me safe, why did he allow Shin to die? If it was truly the Almighty who orchestrated my passage into China, why was I here, cold and hungry and deserted?

In the midst of my thorny sanctuary, I envisioned how many ways I could end my life if I only had the right tool. It was the cruelty of fate that I had no choice but to live. And then, while images of quick and easy suicide played through my mind, the taunting voice of my father's torturer echoed in my memory:

"Song Hyun-Ki hanged himself less than an hour ago, a coward in death just like he was in life."

I stood up. I wouldn't follow in my father's path. I wouldn't shirk away from my destiny, be it torture or sanctuary. I would face my future, whatever it held.

I prayed for protection and stepped out of my thorny retreat. I looked ahead and sucked in my breath. There, less than a hundred meters away, stood a house with a cross hanging in the window, lit by a small candle and scarcely revealed behind a thin curtain.

I stumbled uphill toward the hope of shelter. I realized that this building could be a trap of the Chinese border patrolmen designed to hunt down desperate refugees. But I had no other choice. I stepped up to the house and knocked on the door.

A young man opened it. He was Korean, as was the teenage girl and the older man who stood behind him. As soon as they let me in, all three of them set to work. The younger man examined the blood stain on my coat as he helped me out of it but said nothing. The older man handed me a blanket to wrap around my shivering body. The girl started a fire and gave me a rag to clean my face. A few minutes later she passed me a bowl of rice and broth, which filled the hollow emptiness in my stomach and warmed my aching limbs. After I ate, she guided me to a bed in a room set apart from the main living area. "Please try to rest. Tomorrow, when you have the strength, you can tell us about yourself."

When I saw the bed, covered with a faded quilt and soft feather pillow, all laid out and prepared as if these people had anticipated my arrival for days, I didn't know how to respond. The girl took me by the hand and led me into my new room.

"I can help you brush your hair," she offered. I had no voice, so I just nodded. I hadn't brushed my hair in nine years.

"My name is Kim So-Young." After So-Young helped me out of my prison clothes and into a faded nightgown, she sat on the bed behind me and worked the knots out of my hair.

"I am Song Chung-Cha," I croaked through my parched throat. I was embarrassed to have this girl touch my hair, which was occasionally whacked off to keep its length manageable but otherwise hadn't been kept up for almost a decade. I cringed at So-Young's gentle touch, but the idea of being left alone in this large upholstered room was even more frightening than the thought of So-Young discovering or even contracting my lice.

"Where do you come from?" So-Young asked. For a moment I froze, thinking that I would have to invent a convincing lie. "I mean, where did you live before you were sent to camp?" she added, reminding me that my hosts would have noticed my prison uniform when I first took off Shin's bloody coat.

"I lived in the North Hamyong province." For the first time I realized how strange it was that even my childhood friend Mee-Kyong from the garment factory never knew the name of my hometown. When we were first incarcerated, we were taught that we no longer had a history or a heritage. We were prisoners. Camp 22 was the closest thing to home we would ever know. "That was a long time ago."

"What town in North Hamyong did you use to live in?" So-Young questioned.

"Hasambong."

So-Young held the brush above my head. "Song Chung-Cha?" she repeated. "From Hasambong?"

Her reaction startled me. So-Young jumped up. "Are you related to Song Hyun-Ki?" So-Young pressed, unable to maintain her whisper.

I froze when I heard my father's name spoken in this Chinese home. I nodded in confusion. So-Young ran out of the room. "Our new guest is from Hasambong," I heard her announce in a musical voice. "She is related to Song Hyun-Ki!"

Mr. Kim, So-Young's father, came and stood at my doorway, his lips drooping down to the floor. To judge by his reaction alone, I would have thought being related to Song Hyun-Ki was a grave crime, yet So-Young was smiling brightly at me. The younger man stood outside my room, staring at the floor. I endured so much as a prisoner that I didn't even think to be embarrassed to be seen by these men in nightclothes.

"You came from Hasambong?" Mr. Kim was bald and had a round face, and although he was not obese, he was the most ample man I had ever seen in person. The only portlier individual I knew of was the Dear Leader himself.

"Yes, I grew up in Hasambong." I glanced from one figure to another. The younger man stood blushing, while So-Young clasped her hands and looked from me to her father. Mr. Kim stood with his arms crossed and eyebrows knit together.

"You know Song Hyun-Ki?" asked Mr. Kim. His authoritative voice echoed his disapproval against the four walls of the house.

"He was my father." So-Young gasped aloud. Mr. Kim jerked his head to the side, indicating that we should follow him to the living room. We all sat around the fire.

"We haven't heard any reports regarding Song Hyun-Ki in many years, ever since his arrest. How long ago was that?"

"Nine years." I kept my eyes to the floor. I didn't know how these individuals knew of my father, but I wouldn't be the one to tell them of his fate.

"That long ago?" exclaimed the younger man. "You must have been nothing more than a child then!" He stared at me until Mr. Kim cleared his throat.

"I was twelve."

"And your father?" pressed Mr. Kim. "What has happened to our donkey?"

I didn't understand the phrase, but I knew that – regardless of who they thought he was – I couldn't tell these people the truth about Father's death. "He died in detainment about two weeks after his arrest." Both men nodded their heads. So-Young's smile vanished and she blinked her wide eyes.

I had so many questions. I wanted to ask how these people from across the border knew of my family, but Mr. Kim stood up without warning. "You have undoubtedly had a long journey. You will sleep now." Mr. Kim cast an authoritative glance at his daughter. I caught the younger man's eye, but he shook his head.

My limbs were exhausted, but my heart was weighed down with questions. I went into my room and stretched out on my soft bed. How I ached for the chance to lose myself in a warm and comforting sleep, to momentarily forget that everyone I had ever cared for – or who had ever cared for me – was dead. But my mind was racing. Who were these strangers, and how did they know about my father? How had they heard of his arrest so many years ago when we lived across such a tightly controlled border?

In the other room, I heard Mr. Kim and the other man talking late into the night. I couldn't make out what they said, but there was no mistaking the intensity in their voices.

THE GIFT

"So is the word that goes out from my mouth: It will not return to me empty, but will accomplish what I desire and achieve the purpose for which I sent it." Isaiah 55:11

"Where is everybody?" I asked So-Young when I got out of bed the middle of the next day. Still in my nightgown, I entered the main living room and found my teenage hostess alone washing dishes at the basin sink.

"Good morning." So-Young turned her face away and hid her smile.

"Where is everybody?" I repeated. So-Young stared at the pan she was scrubbing, blushing until the red crept all the way down her neck.

"Nowhere." So-Young closed her lips together. As she focused on scouring the pot, a giggle crept up her throat. I couldn't remember the last time I laughed, perhaps some time with Mee-Kyong before her pregnancy.

I didn't ask So-Young any more questions. I took the cup of tea she handed me and warmed my face in the steam. "Are you hungry?" So-Young asked.

"Yes, very." I sat down at the table. So-Young stopped washing dishes and cracked a few eggs into her wok. A few minutes later, she placed a full plate on the table then sat down across from me. "My father keeps some chickens out back." So-Young's explanation wasn't necessary; if the chickens hadn't been clucking all morning long I would still be in bed.

"Did you sleep well?" I nodded with my mouth full, feeling boorish. My experience in labor camp didn't prepare me for polite mealtime conversations. Although I filled myself on rice and broth the night before, I was famished.

"My father should be returning soon." It seemed clear that So-Young was the woman of the house. I wondered what became of her mother, and how this beautiful girl managed to remain so joyful and radiant with the burden of running a home on her shoulders.

"And the young man?" I inquired. "Is he your brother?"

"Kwan?" So-Young's dark eyes grew large. "My brother?" So-Young stifled another giggle and turned away, hiding her flushed cheeks. She didn't offer any further explanation.

"How long have you lived here?"

"I've forgotten." So-Young poured me another cup of tea. "I was very young when my father and I moved to Sanhe."

I had more questions, but the front door opened. So-Young jumped up. She raised her eyebrow at her father. Mr. Kim nodded his head almost imperceptibly, although he didn't return her smile. So-Young looked at Kwan and blushed once more. "So then you were able to find it?" she asked him.

Mr. Kim cleared his throat. "Come with me, Daughter. I need your help with the chickens." So-Young looked at her father, then at me, then at Kwan. Her wide and expectant eyes lowered, and her thin shoulders fell toward the floor. She didn't argue with her father, but So-Young bit her lip as she followed Mr. Kim to the chicken coop out back. Before she closed the door behind her, she glanced back at Kwan with a pout.

Kwan stood staring at me, scratching his elbow and drooping his head. Kwan was a little too tall and much too skinny to be handsome. He wore wiry glasses and looked like he needed some sunshine to help color his pallid face.

Kwan lowered himself into the same chair So-Young was sitting in a moment earlier. He reached in his coat.

"I have a … a present for you." Kwan fumbled in his pocket for a moment, and then he took out a black leather book. "Do you recognize this?"

"Yes." I picked up the Bible and turned it around in my hands. "My father had one like it." I wondered how many Korean Bibles with study notes were in this region. I couldn't understand why Kwan's eyes shone or why his lanky frame leaned toward me so expectantly.

"Don't you see?" Kwan rubbed his hands together. "It is your Father's!"

I was glad that I was already sitting down. I didn't know what to ask Kwan first. The mysterious link that somehow connected my father to these strangers in China was as frightening as it was baffling.

"Sister Chung-Cha." Kwan blinked hard as he stared at my empty breakfast plate. "You were very young when you father was arrested. He probably never had the chance to tell you of his work for the Lord."

"What do you mean?" I never wondered until now why my father was given a study Bible when most pastors and evangelists in North Korea probably didn't have a New Testament. I resented that Kwan knew more about this Bible and my father's history than I did.

"Before his arrest," Kwan explained, "I was privileged to meet your father over a dozen times."

I thought for a moment that this might all be a huge mistake. Perhaps there was another Christian man with a similar name who also happened to live in our small village. Yet there was Father's Bible before me, the one he so deeply cherished. There was the same black leather binding, the same small print, the same bent corner on the back cover.

"Are you from Hasambong?" I flipped the Bible over and back again in my shaking hands, trying to perceive whatever secrets it contained.

"No." Kwan shook his head. "I've never been across the border myself. It was your father who came here to us."

"Here? To China?" I couldn't remember what So-Young called their town earlier.

"There is so much you were never able to learn." Kwan took off his glasses and wiped them with his sleeve. "Your father often spoke about you, you know. He regretted not being able to tell you about his work as a donkey." I stared at the teacup in front of me so I didn't have to meet Kwan's gaze. I was embarrassed to admit I had no idea what he was talking about. "Your father was the only Bible smuggler I know who also had a young child. Most donkeys I've met are unmarried. The fewer attachments, the better. Many times Mr. Kim urged your father to choose a less risky vocation to serve the underground church, but your father would never listen to his warnings."

Unwillingly I heard Agent Lee's voice in my head: *"What a pity your father loves his silly god more than you."*

"Song Hyung-Ki was a brave man." Kwan scratched his black hair. "Perhaps the bravest man I've ever known."

I squared my shoulders, vowing that I would never tell Kwan and his friends what really happened to Father in the detainment center. It still didn't seem possible that the father I knew and revered as a child led such a secret life. I looked around the room at the chair Father might have sat in, the fire where he would have warmed himself after his dangerous trek across the Tumen River. A question came to me. "Did Mother know?"

Kwan shook his head. "Hyun-Ki didn't want to worry her any more than necessary. From what your father said, it sounded like she was anxious enough without knowing of your father's dangerous work. Hyun-Ki completed all of his journeys by night while you and your mother were sleeping." I thought back to the times when I was certain I heard Father come in during the early morning hours. I always assumed he was outside meditating under the stars of Hasambong that he and I both loved so much. I never imagined that he went to a foreign country and back.

"How did he keep from getting caught?" I sipped my tea, trying to stop myself from shaking.

"Hyun-Ki was remarkably blessed, as though he was protected by the archangel himself." Kwan rubbed the top of his thigh. "Most other donkeys I've known only manage to make the journey two or three times. It is very dangerous." I thought about the night Shin was killed crossing the border.

"But Father wasn't even arrested for smuggling Bibles." I shuddered. How much more would our family have suffered if Father was caught crossing the border with Bibles?

Kwan cracked his knuckle. "The last time we saw him, your father told us that he didn't know how many more trips he could make. We all knew that it was just a matter of time before Hyun-Ki was arrested for his work as a donkey. Too many Koreans were being caught with Bibles and interrogated for him to stay safe for much longer." Kwan stretched his bony legs under the table. "Actually, we were all relieved to learn that Hyun-Ki was arrested by the inspections unit. We hoped that your family's punishment would be less severe than if he were discovered across the border."

I thought about my parents' argument the night the People's Safety Agency barged into our cabin. "Do you think he meant to be caught?"

"It's possible." Kwan scratched his smooth face. "Maybe he decided it was safer that way for you and your mother. But I never knew your father to be afraid of anything." For the first time it sounded like Kwan was talking about the same Father I remembered from my childhood. "Hyun-Ki was the only donkey who refused to adopt an alias. He believed that to use a different name when he crossed the border would reveal fear and embarrassment of the gospel."

The mention of pseudonyms reminded me of the Bible smuggler my father revered so much. "Have you ever heard of a man called Moses?" Immediately, Kwan's smile disappeared and his eyes narrowed. He leaned his head close to mine.

"Never mention that name," Kwan hissed. I couldn't tell if he was frightened or angry.

I recoiled in surprise. "I'm sorry."

Kwan sat back in his chair. "There are some things that you should not ask. It's for your own safety," Kwan assured me with a heavy sigh.

UNSPOKEN

*"Do not be quick with your mouth, do not be hasty in your heart
to utter anything before God." Ecclesiastes 5:2*

"May I come in?"

I looked up and was surprised to see Kwan standing in the
doorway to my room. "Am I interrupting your study?" Kwan
glanced at my father's Bible lying open on my lap.

"No, I was just reading." I was curious to know what Kwan
was doing in my room. For the past three weeks at the safe
house if either Kwan or Mr. Kim had a message for me, they
relied on So-Young to deliver it. In such a short time, So-
Young became a dear friend. I hated the thought of leaving her
in only a few days. My time at Mr. Kim's safe house passed
much too quickly.

"Are you ready for your journey?" I wondered if Kwan came
to my room just to chat.

"I think I have everything I need." I gestured to my duffel
bag. "The clothes So-Young found will fit after a little altering.
And I hear that Mrs. Cho is an excellent seamstress."

"So they say." Kwan sat on the edge of my bed. At first he
stared at his knobby hands that rested on his knees. Then he
turned and gazed at my half-filled suitcase. "You will be a great
blessing to her."

I didn't know how to respond. I wished for some way to
keep my hands occupied.

"How many children did you say Mrs. Cho cares for?" I
picked some imaginary lint off of the duffel bag and smoothed
So-Young's dress that I was wearing.

"At least twenty." Kwan cleared his throat. "Maybe more by
now. I don't know how she has been able to keep up with all of

them for so long without any help. You must be an answer to many prayers offered up to heaven on her behalf."

"There's such a need." I remembered when I first heard about Mrs. Cho. About one week after I arrived at the safe house, I woke up in the middle of the night to the sound of an almost catlike crying. The next morning I saw So-Young in the common living area. She was caring for newborn twin girls. Since I was a guest in the safe house, Mr. Kim didn't allow me speak with any of the other refugees who came seeking help. He also wouldn't let me ask questions about anything else going on around me. It was for my own safety, Mr. Kim assured me. I was curious about the babies, but I couldn't talk about them until So-Young and I were left alone later that day.

"Who is their mother?" I asked So-Young.

"We don't know." She shrugged her delicate shoulders. "By the time we woke up to their crying, the person who dropped them off was gone." So-Young pursed her lips into a tight little ring as she cradled one of the twins. "People drop their babies off here fairly often."

"Why?" I rubbed my cheek against the baby who was asleep drooling on my shoulder. What would bring anyone to abandon such a helpless creature?

"The mothers are almost all refugees from North Korea." So-Young shifted the child in her arms. "The fathers are either Korean or Chinese. It doesn't really matter. Either way, the babies will never be accepted here in Sanhe."

"What happens to them?" I knew that adult defectors captured in China were immediately sent back to North Korea to face their punishment. I never thought about the children they might bear while they were on foreign soil.

"Some are abandoned, others are killed at birth. Of course, many women try to raise their infants, but if the mother is repatriated, her children will be sent back with her. Every once in a while the babies find their way to our door, just like these angels."

I never saw So-Young look so content as she did at that moment. A twinge of loneliness pierced my heart when I remembered my own mother. In all of my memories, Mother never looked at me with such gentleness and love. Perhaps our homeland, which stole away our freedom long before we saw the confines of Camp 22, kept her from being the mother she might have been, the mother I now longed for with a poignant heaviness.

"Sister So-Young." I didn't want to be so blunt, but there was no tactful way to voice my question. "Where is your mother?"

So-Young wiggled her finger in front of the little girl's face but stopped looking at her. "I don't remember my mother."

"What happened?"

So-Young hung her head. "My father won't tell me."

I thought about Mr. Kim and tried to guess his reasoning. "Why not?"

So-Young smoothed out her jet-black hair. "I don't ask him anymore. He just tells me that he doesn't want to talk about her. Sometimes I wonder if she died giving birth to me. But why wouldn't Father say so?" An uncharacteristic whine crept into So-Young's voice.

"I'm sorry," I apologized. "I wasn't trying to ..."

"I know." So-Young smiled at me. "With so much work going on at the safe house, I don't really have time to miss a woman I can't remember."

I have to admit, beloved daughter, that as So-Young and I talked, I never thought about becoming a mother myself, about loving a child so dearly, about adoring someone who might never even remember my face ...

I knew So-Young was trying to be cheerful, but I still regretted bringing up such a sensitive subject. "And what about your mother?" So-Young asked me.

"I remember her," I admitted. "I know she loved me, but I have very few fond memories left of her."

"She is still in prison camp, then?" The baby in So-Young's arms began to fuss.

I shook my head. "She died just a few weeks after we arrived there."

"I am sorry to hear that." So-Young bounced the upset little girl in her arms.

"What will you do with the twins?" I was relieved to change the subject. For a moment, I hoped that So-Young would say we would keep the babies. In all my life, I had never smelled anything so fresh and pure and innocent as the little girl I now cradled in my arms.

"We have a contact in South Korea." So-Young rubbed the baby's back. "My father has already notified her. She has an orphanage in Seoul devoted to little ones like these."

"So this woman will come and pick the girls up?"

"No, not at all." So-Young understood much better than I that, although these children were born on Chinese soil, they would never be granted the rights of Chinese citizens or the legal ability to move around from country to country. "There is an entire network established to get the babies to South Korea."

It was only two days later when an old woman arrived at the safe house. She was the first of many links, I gathered, to transport the twins safely to the orphanage in Seoul. I was in my room, and as I had been instructed I did not come out. Still, I couldn't keep from overhearing the conversation as the baby girls were placed in the woman's care on the other side of my bedroom door.

"I wish you safety and speed on your journey," Mr. Kim told the stranger. "May you have ample strength for the road ahead of you." I never heard Mr. Kim speak so kindly to anyone in the safe house before, and for a moment I wondered if the voice I heard truly belonged to my benefactor.

"The Lord Almighty will tend to my old arthritic bones," declared the lady. "I've made this journey many times."

"I have not forgotten, Sister," responded Mr. Kim.

"It is Mrs. Cho that needs your prayers more than I." The woman wouldn't know that I was listening behind my closed door, a stranger who shouldn't have even heard the identity of this South Korean worker. "Caring for almost two dozen children and she nearly eighty. It is too much work for one woman alone."

"The Lord gives our sister in Seoul remarkable strength," Mr. Kim observed.

"That he does," admitted the courier, "but what Mrs. Cho really needs is a strong girl to help her care for so many babies."

A few mornings later So-Young shook me awake at dawn.

"Wake up, Sister!" she exclaimed.

"What is it?" I asked, hoping my voice didn't sound as cross as I felt at having been aroused from my sleep.

"Father asked me to talk to you." So-Young didn't pause for breath. "Remember the woman I told you about? The one who runs an orphanage in South Korea? She needs help. She needs someone to help look after her babies. Father says he thinks you should consider it." So-Young prattled on while I tried to open my eyes.

"She can provide you with room and board. Imagine it! You'd be in Seoul. You'd be safe there, and no one could ever send you back to North Korea again. Can you believe it? Mrs. Cho has already offered to provide for your passage. It's a long journey, of course, but you know, God protected you from so many things in your past. Why wouldn't he just keep on watching over you now?"

And so it was decided that in a fortnight I would travel to the interior of China with Mrs. Cho's many anonymous escorts. I would make the journey by car, train, and foot all the way to Vietnam and then take a boat to South Korea. The trek sounded arduous, but I was assured that Mrs. Cho aided so many refugees along that path before that I had very little to worry about. Boredom and exhaustion would probably be the biggest threats to my well-being.

The hardest part about leaving Sanhe would be saying good-bye to So-Young. More than once Mr. Kim came in to my room late at night to send So-Young off to bed. I loved hearing So-Young's stories about the people she knew in Sanhe. Her life seemed to be so simple, so normal.

"What do you do when you go to the market?" I asked. There were no markets in Hasambong when I was a child. I listened with interest to So-Young's accounts of bargaining and bartering.

"What happens when you go to your house church?" So-Young and I sat side by side on my bed, swinging our feet over the edge. It took So-Young at least an hour to answer all my questions about Christians in China. Even my father, as far as I knew, had never attended a real church service, although there were many things about my father that I was still learning.

I sometimes worried that my incessant questions were burdensome, but So-Young assured me she was grateful for someone to talk to. "My father doesn't like to 'squander words,' as he puts it."

"I believe that," I whispered back.

"It's nice having another younger person to talk to."

"Kwan's young." I studied my friend to gauge her reaction. So-Young giggled but said nothing.

"The house will seem so empty once you leave for Seoul," So-Young confessed after she stopped blushing.

"At least your father won't yell at you for staying up late anymore." So-Young giggled again. It was a sweet, musical sound, and for a moment I pretended that I was like So-Young: a normal girl living in a normal city, a girl whose body wasn't scarred from years of torture and mistreatment, a girl who hadn't spent years of her life without the sound of laughter. I wondered if I would laugh once I was safe in South Korea.

And now, just two days before my voyage, Kwan was sitting on my bed cracking his knuckles, opening his mouth every few moments and then closing it again.

"So-Young will miss you." Kwan squinted his eyes behind his thick glasses.

"I'll miss her too."

Another minute of strained silence passed, then So-Young came into the safe house carrying a small basket full of eggs. "Good-evening!" she sang out, and then stopped when she saw Kwan on my bed. She stared at him in surprise. Kwan cleared his throat, adjusted his glasses, and left my room without taking his eyes off of the floor. So-Young watched him retreat then glanced at me. Somehow I felt I owed So-Young an explanation, but I couldn't think of anything to say.

So-Young swallowed. "I just wanted to tell you that I'm going over to Pastor Tong's house to help him care for his mother. It might be a while." Before I could think of an appropriate response, So-Young left the safe house once again.

I sat on my bed with my father's Bible on my lap, fearful that So-Young was hurt, wondering if Kwan would return, thinking about the long journey ahead of me. When half an hour passed and Kwan didn't come back, I finally stretched out under my blankets. Nightfall was still several hours away, but it wasn't long before I fell asleep.

THE CALL

"It is too small a thing for you to be my servant to restore the tribes of Jacob ... I will also make you a light for the Gentiles, that you may bring my salvation to the ends of the earth."
Isaiah 49:6

"Don't touch me!"

The frantic words woke me up with a start. My door was closed, and I wasn't allowed to peek into the common living area to see what was happening.

"Get your hands off me!" a woman shrieked. "Don't come any closer!"

I heard something fall to the ground. "Where is So-Young?" Mr. Kim demanded.

"With Pastor's mother," answered Kwan. I sat up in bed.

"I don't need your help!" shouted the woman.

"We can give you a safe place to stay."

"Get away from me!" she screamed again. I recognized the terror in her voice and remembered my own panic when I escaped Camp 22 with Shin.

"She won't listen to us."

"Do you want me to bring So-Young?" Kwan asked.

"You'll have to. Tell her we need her here."

"I am going to find someone who can help you," Kwan said. I heard intermittent cries, but the woman didn't appear to be struggling as vigorously as at first.

It was times like these when I hated the rules of the safe house. Who was Mr. Kim to determine when I could or couldn't help someone in need? If a woman suffered so much at the hands of her male captors, how did Mr. Kim and Kwan expect her to trust any man at all? I was glad when Kwan left to get So-

Young, and I hoped So-Young's feminine grace would help reassure the battered woman.

Several minutes passed in silence. I opened my father's Bible, and I was startled by the sound of broken glass. "Stay away from me!" I heard a loud thud followed by Mr. Kim's grunt. I couldn't stand sitting idly anymore behind my closed doors, so I hurried into the main part of the house. Mr. Kim was lying on the floor, his head bleeding. A haggard woman in prison clothes crouched in the corner with a cracked bowl in her hand.

"What are you doing?" Mr. Kim barked when he saw me. The woman hugged herself, shivering and grunting like a trapped animal. I turned my back to Mr. Kim and addressed her.

"I am Song Chung-Cha." I figured that this prisoner's deep scars were more significant than Mr. Kim's displeasure.

The woman rocked back and forth. My words didn't calm her in any way. "I came here a few weeks ago," I explained. "I was a prisoner too." The woman let out a tiny sigh but still didn't say anything.

"These people have been good to me. No one here would ever hurt you." The woman winced. I wondered what else I could say to help her.

"You must be hungry." The woman nodded. Mr. Kim picked up a bowl of stew that was already on the table, but when the woman saw him approaching with it, she wrapped her arms around her chest and mumbled softly to herself.

I understood the woman's misery all too well. I took the bowl from Mr. Kim. "You should eat this now." With my own hand, I brought a spoonful of broth to the woman's cracked lips. "You don't need to be afraid anymore. You're safe here with us."

The woman reached out for the bowl with trembling hands. "You're safe," I whispered to her again.

When I turned around, Kwan and So-Young were standing in the doorway. With a nod of understanding between themselves, Kwan and Mr. Kim left the common room. So-Young came to my side and helped me care for our new guest.

That evening I gave up my own chamber and joined So-Young in her room, which was really just a corner of the common area separated by a bamboo partition. Mr. Kim was far from happy about the arrangement. "It's the best we can do for now," he grumbled to So-Young, "but I don't want you staying up late. You still have to wake up early to tend the chickens."

"Yes, Father." So-Young stretched out on her small mattress next to me and sighed with satisfaction. "Now you know why I love my work here," she remarked once Mr. Kim left. For the first time, I understood the contentment and peace that radiated from So-Young. In all my life, I'm not sure I ever knew greater fulfillment. My joy was matched only by my exhaustion.

"It was a wonderful feeling." I thought about the woman we just helped. "But don't you ever get tired?" It seemed like for the past three weeks I did very little but sleep and read my father's Bible while So-Young was up before dawn. In addition to managing the safe house and weaving baskets to sell, So-Young often went into town on errands of mercy.

"I do grow weary sometimes," So-Young admitted, "but I know that God has called me to this work, and so I trust him to give me the strength I need each day."

I grew pensive at So-Young's comment. Although I feared my question would sound foolish, I ventured, "How do you know that you are called here?"

"At the safe house?" So-Young asked. "Where else would I go? Besides, there's nothing in the world I would rather be doing than serving here."

"Honestly?" I turned over to look at So-Young better. "Nothing at all?"

"Well, I hope one day to marry and have a family of my own." So-Young stifled a giggle. "But that's still several years away." I relished So-Young's youthful naiveté, yet envied her spiritual maturity.

"Have you been thinking about Mrs. Cho's orphanage?" So-Young asked perceptively.

I nodded.

"Do you feel like God might be calling you somewhere else to minister?"

"I don't know. I've read so much in my father's Bible about God's love for children, that true religion is to take care of orphans. It even says that God Himself is the Father of the fatherless. But I'm not sure I would be able to do that sort of work. I barely had a childhood of my own, and I've never cared for kids before in my life. What could I possibly do to help them?"

"You can offer them your love," So-Young answered with wide-eyed simplicity. "And your heart. Just think of all the hurting souls you could bless!" I imagined that So-Young would blossom and flourish wherever she went. I, on the other hand, would probably be nothing more than an extra limb at Mrs. Cho's orphanage. Certainly there were more qualified young woman who could serve in my place.

"What do you want to be doing?" When I stared at So-Young blankly, she rephrased her question. "If you could choose your destiny, what would it be?" The words were like a foreign language to me. Up until I arrived at the safe house, I wasn't even free to choose my own clothing or food. I mulled over So-Young's question in silence, but before I had the chance to answer, Mr. Kim appeared at the opening in the bamboo partition.

"Daughter, it is past time you went to sleep. Kwan and I would like to have a word right now with our guest."

I glanced at So-Young. She kept her gaze on the quilted blanket. I followed Mr. Kim to the common area where Kwan was sitting on a wooden stool cracking his knuckles.

Once I was situated across from both men, Mr. Kim cleared his throat. "Sister Chung-Cha, as a guest in our safe house, you were expected to abide by certain rules and regulations." I picked at my nails in embarrassment. "These rules are for your own protection. This safe house is meant to be a haven, a refuge for the weary. We do not ask our guests to serve alongside us, only to let us serve them."

I winced. "Your actions this evening showed me two things." I wondered how it was that Mr. Kim would risk his personal safety to serve others in the name of Christ, yet he had never once smiled in my presence. "First, it revealed to me that your years spent in the labor camps stripped you of your ability to submit to any sort of authority." For a moment, I feared that Mr. Kim was going to forbid me from traveling to Seoul in a few days. He coughed before continuing. "Nevertheless, I am forced to admit that your actions tonight also showed me that the trials of your past enable you to minister effectively and compassionately to the refugees we serve here."

For the first time I dared to glance into Mr. Kim's stern face. Out of the corner of my eye I saw Kwan smiling at me broadly, and after receiving an affirmative grunt from Mr. Kim he spoke. "What Mr. Kim is saying is that there are certain defectors who come to our doors that need someone like you, someone who has gone through the same trials they have, someone who has suffered at the hands of the same guards they have." I was humiliated at this allusion to my own abusive past. Nevertheless, my heart was racing as I understood what these two men were saying.

"And so," Kwan concluded, "Mr. Kim and I would like you to reconsider your journey to Mrs. Cho's orphanage. Of course, if you feel God leading you to Seoul, you have our blessing to go. But if you sense the Lord is preparing you for a ministry here alongside us at the safe house, we would welcome you as our sister and fellow servant."

I tried unsuccessfully to hide my grin. "I want to stay here!"

Mr. Kim grimaced. "Think it through. If you go to South Korea, you will be safe. You can become a citizen. The South Korean government gives people like you a stipend to live off of, at least at first. No one will ever try to deport you." I couldn't tell if Mr. Kim wanted to scare me away from staying in Sanhe, or if he only wanted me to be aware of the dangers involved. "If you remain here, you are taking a great risk. If you are caught by the police, they will send you back to the prison camps."

I don't know where my confidence came from, but I squared my shoulders and declared, "God has led me here safely. I don't expect that he will forsake me now."

So-Young, who was standing at the opening of her partition unnoticed, squealed with delight, then ran in and embraced me. "Sister!" she exclaimed. Mr. Kim turned away with a frown, but Kwan watched me intently, with a look that left me perplexed for the rest of the night and into the following days and weeks.

SEASONS

"As long as the earth endures, seedtime and harvest, cold and heat, summer and winter, day and night will never cease."
Genesis 8:22

Spring crept upon the Jilin Province. Each day, dawn awakened the lush Sanhe countryside a little earlier than the day before. The sparrows in the woods behind our home warbled, and the warm winds from the southwest melted away the last of the snow and ice.

As I regained my strength little by little, I took over most of the domestic duties at the safe house, allowing So-Young more time to tend to the sick and impoverished in Sanhe. Mr. Kim and Kwan, in addition to their daytime employment, were working to build an extension off the safe house that would provide two extra rooms for refugees. The Tumen River was running quickly now, nearly overflowing its banks with the influx of melted snow from the mountain streams. Not many defectors dared ford the river at its peak in the springtime months. But even though we saw very few new refugees, we had plenty of work to keep up around the safe house.

When summer arrived, the clammy winds brought a higher than expected infestation of mosquitoes throughout Sanhe. Several more Korean babies were left on our doorstep during those hot and muggy months. And although I vividly remember the first two twin girls we cared for, I don't recall many of the nameless others who arrived in baskets outside our door.

So-Young and I watched over the infants until Mrs. Cho's escorts came to carry them on the long journey to South Korea. Mrs. Cho was disappointed that I didn't come to work with her at the orphanage but assured me in a warm and encouraging letter that I would be welcome to join her in Seoul if I ever reconsidered. Mrs. Cho alluded to the risks I faced by staying in Sanhe, and I couldn't discredit her warnings. The Chinese police were constantly trying to capture Korean nationals and send us back to our homeland.

My safe-house family never ignored these dangers. Mr. Kim kept his cellular phone charged and never went anywhere without it. He had an anonymous contact who agreed to warn him of impending police raids. Mr. Kim made me and any other refugees at the safe house practice hiding. If the home was raided, we needed to disappear in a matter of seconds. He and Kwan built a trap door leading to a small cellar on the side of the safe house in case of a surprise visit from the Chinese police.

When I was not busy cooking or cleaning for my safe-house family, I worked at home. So-Young taught me to weave baskets that the Kims sold to help pay for the safe house's vast expenses. I wished I could join So-Young on her endless errands of mercy, but without proper papers it wasn't safe for me to be seen around Sanhe. Some of the citizens there would be glad to turn me over to the Chinese police for the promised bribe price.

During those long and busy summer months, the fields around the safe house grew more and more inviting. With my strength slowly returning after years of malnourishment and intermittent torture, I wanted nothing more than to be outside. Unfortunately, because the Sanhe police would deport me back to North Korea if they found out where I was from, Mr. Kim didn't let me leave the safe house alone. My most coveted luxury became the short walks I took with Kwan in the evenings when he came home from work. We usually strolled in back of the safe house, never tarrying far, and I took So-Young's identification papers with me in case we were stopped. Although these outings didn't allow me to wander all over and explore the vast forests and hillsides surrounding Sanhe, they were a much appreciated reprieve from the four walls of the safe house that made up the rest of my Sanhe existence.

Kwan was a pleasant chaperone, and I enjoyed spending my evenings with him. Time passed too quickly on our walks together. Kwan asked me many questions about my childhood, especially about my father. It didn't take long for me to realize that Father was as great a hero to Kwan as he once was to me. I told Kwan about Father as I remembered him before his arrest: a doting parent, a patient teacher, a passionate scholar. Kwan, in return, told me about my father's work as a donkey, a Scripture smuggler who brought more Bibles into North Hamyong Province than anyone else Kwan knew of. Remembering Kwan's warning on our first morning together, I never mentioned Moses again, but I asked myself if this great hero was the link that connected my father to my safe-house family. I wondered if one day I might meet him.

"How did you ever get my father's Bible?" I asked Kwan one evening as we strolled along the forested area behind the safe house.

Kwan pulled aside a leafy branch and held it out for me as I passed. "On his last journey here, your father told us that he might not be able to return to Sanhe for a while." I focused on Kwan's voice, trying to remember each word exactly as he uttered it. Like so many other times when Kwan spoke about my father, I imagined I was learning about him for the very first time.

"Hyun-Ki told us that the inspections unit was coming to Hasambong. Your father knew that his Bible wouldn't be safe in your home, so he asked us to keep it for him until he returned to Sanhe again."

"Do you think he was scared?" I tried to remember a time when I had seen my father afraid.

Kwan shook his head. "Not scared. But Korean study Bibles are very scarce, and I guess your father didn't want such a precious gift to be confiscated."

"So he brought the Bible here?"

Kwan nodded. "Hyun-Ki loaned it to us until he could return again to Sanhe. But then when we learned of your father's arrest, we had to admit there was little chance of his survival. If we knew anything at all about Hyun-Ki, it was that he would keep on preaching the gospel until he drew his last breath." Kwan straightened his shoulders and lifted his chin. So far I kept my promise to never divulge the truth behind Father's fate. As far as Kwan and the Kims knew, Father died of torture in the underground detainment center. I wouldn't bring myself to dishonor my father's memory, especially amongst those who loved and respected him so deeply, by telling them what really happened to Father in those underground chambers of Camp 22.

Kwan stared at the cluster of wildflowers by our feet. "Your father was an amazing man."

"I know." I wondered what Kwan would say if I told him the full truth. I looked back over my shoulder to see how far we had meandered from the safe house.

Kwan was quiet, and in unspoken agreement we both turned around to go back home. I couldn't guess what Kwan was thinking about. I looked in the distance at the purple and yellow flowers that covered the hillside. I thought of my father who always adored God's creation.

"Do you see these mountains, righteous daughter?" Father once asked me, pointing to the Hasambong range that surrounded our home on nearly every side. "No matter how corrupt man becomes, he still can't tarnish the beauty of God's world. It is a constant reminder to us of our Creator's faithfulness and power, even in spite of the world's ever-increasing wickedness."

I couldn't remember whether it was years, or months, or only weeks later that I learned my father died a shameful death after denying the Savior he once worshiped so passionately.

"There's more to the story, you know." Kwan had been so quiet that the sound of his voice made me jump.

"I'm sorry." Kwan apologized and cracked a knuckle. "I didn't mean to startle you." When I didn't respond, Kwan said, "We were discussing your father's Bible."

I didn't feel like talking about my apostate father's precious Scripture anymore, but I couldn't think of any way to change the subject.

"When we heard of his arrest, we guessed that your father would not be returning to us in Sanhe. So Mr. Kim and I both decided that the best way to honor your father's legacy of boldness was to share his Bible with as many as would benefit from it. That single book has gone into North Korea five times and back since your father was taken prisoner. We send it to those who need it most, then when they find it too risky to hold on to, the Bible makes its way back to us in Sanhe."

I tried to think of something to say, but with the events surrounding Father's shameful death so vivid in my memory, the only words that came to mind would have sounded trite and forced. Fortunately, Kwan needed no encouragement to keep up his monologue.

"In all those times, it was never discovered," Kwan remarked. I glanced up at the first traces of a golden sunset. "Most recently, Mr. Kim loaned it to Pastor Tong's son here in Sanhe who was eager to understand the Word more fully. Pastor Tong's family is Korean as well, although they did not come from the north. The morning after you arrived in Sanhe, Mr. Kim and I told the pastor's son that you were here. We all agreed that no one has more claim to that great treasure as Song Hyun-Ki's beautiful daughter."

Kwan looked away and scratched his chin, refusing to speak again for several minutes. I knew that Kwan found me attractive. Yet instead of basking in the attention of this kind and gentle man, I was thinking of a night several months before. It was two days after I agreed to remain at the safe house. So-Young was so excited about my decision to stay that she planned an entire feast to welcome me into her family. She braided my hair with ribbons and barrettes and let me wear one of her best dresses. She was so proud of the overall effect that she ran to a neighbor's house to borrow her small mirror.

"Look!" So-Young held the glass up to my face with a triumphant beam.

I would never have recognized the face that stared back at me from the looking glass. My eyes were large and hollow. My cheeks were gaunt in spite of the several weeks that I spent satisfying myself with So-Young's ample cooking. I looked at least a decade older than my age. My throat constricted when I saw the pale stranger gaping back at me.

My effect at dinner that night, however, was significantly more positive. When I came to the table, Kwan spilled his tea. He grew bright red and made something topple to the floor two more times before we finished eating. Even from Mr. Kim, I imagined a fatherly pride where before I only knew sternness.

As Kwan stared at me the entire dinner long, I wondered if So-Young feared that she had made me a little bit too presentable for my welcoming banquet. Ever since So-Young reacted so strangely when she saw Kwan talking to me in my room, I did my best to ignore Kwan and his awkward glances in my direction. So-Young never admitted her feelings for Kwan to me. Whenever I asked her about their relationship, So-Young found a way to avoid the question or change the subject. "Kwan?" she'd say as carelessly as she could. "He's like an uncle. I grew up with him."

I wasn't fooled. Because of So-Young's obvious affection, I tried to avoid Kwan as much as possible during my first several months in Sanhe. In the safe house, I treated Kwan with nothing more than polite indifference. I didn't want to give him – or So-Young – the impression that there was anything between us other than formal courtesy. But as the warm sunshine grew more and more inviting, as my lungs longed for fresh air and my spirit yearned for the beauty of the Sanhe hillside covered in wildflowers, I spent more and more time with Kwan in the evenings. Strolling beside the Sanhe forests with Kwan, conversation came easily and our time together felt so natural. I found myself avoiding So-Young altogether when my escort and I returned to the safe house.

As the summer solstice came and went and the days once again began to grow colder with the promise of a crisp and early autumn, I couldn't ignore Kwan's ever-increasing attention toward me, even as I pretended to remain unaffected. I didn't allow myself to blush or swoon under his frank approval, but at night when I tried to pray, that day's conversations with Kwan ran through my mind instead. Sometimes I wished I hadn't stayed in Sanhe at all. Instead of appreciating Kwan's flattery and admiration, I feared I was stealing away the happiness that belonged to So-Young.

I was not the only one in Sanhe who regretted the impact my presence was having on So-Young. I was cleaning up the kitchen after dinner one evening when Mr. Kim entered the safe house. After greeting his daughter, he looked at me and cleared his throat.

"I will accompany you on a walk now," Mr. Kim stated. Usually if Kwan was not home by sunset, which came earlier and earlier with each autumn day, I would forgo my evening stroll and content myself reading Father's Bible or chatting with So-Young while we weaved baskets together by the window. I glanced at So-Young, who raised her eyebrows first at her father and then at me. She shrugged slightly and handed me her identity papers.

"Get a coat," Mr. Kim ordered. It wasn't so cold that I needed an extra layer, but I did as I was told and followed Mr. Kim out of the safe house.

"I am worried about my daughter," Mr. Kim declared once we were outside.

His pace was much quicker than Kwan's, and I had to exert myself to keep from falling too far behind. "So-Young? Why are you worried about her?"

"Frankly, I am concerned about the influence that your friendship is having on her."

I thought back over anything I might have said or done in the past few weeks to incur Mr. Kim's mistrust.

"I do not blame you for your past, but I believe I am correct in assuming that you were – forgive me for not putting this more delicately – but that you were misused while you were a prisoner?"

I clenched my hands into fists and dug my fingernails into my palms. "That's a correct assumption." I gritted my teeth and stayed a pace or two behind Mr. Kim.

"So-Young is still a child. She is still quite innocent and ignorant about many things." I wanted to defend myself, but I waited while Mr. Kim expressed his concerns. "My daughter loves you dearly." I bristled at the obvious disappointment I heard in his voice. For the first time I wondered if my invitation to stay at the safe house was more Kwan's idea than Mr. Kim's. Mr. Kim cleared his throat as we circled around to the trail that would lead us back behind the chicken coop. "Although I appreciate your work here, I need to tell you that it would not be a welcomed event if you tainted So-Young's mind with colorful images or depictions of your more sullied past."

When I was certain that Mr. Kim was waiting for my response, I took a deep breath and tried to keep my voice from wavering. "I would never hurt So-Young or compromise her innocence." I swallowed several times to will away the lump in my throat. "I can assure you that I would never talk to her about this particular aspect of my history." I paused to steady my voice, not daring to look at Mr. Kim. "So-Young is a treasure." I spoke rapidly before my constricting throat betrayed my mortification. "I beg you to believe me when I tell you that I would never intentionally harm her in any way."

"It's not the intentional harm that concerns me." I was thankful when the safe house came into view, and I began to walk faster to reach its sheltering refuge. "It's the unintentional," Mr. Kim added under his breath.

AWAKENING

"Daughters of Jerusalem, I charge you by the gazelles and by the does of the field: Do not arouse or awaken love until it so desires." Song of Songs 3:5

"Sister Chung-Cha?" I hugged my sweater tight around me to ward off the crisp October wind. I glanced at Kwan out of the corner of my eye. His shoulders were hunched over, and he scratched his cheek while casting a furtive glance in my direction. "Can I ask you a delicate question?"

"Of course." I tried to sound indifferent. I didn't realize I was speeding up until I looked back and saw Kwan several paces behind me, cracking his knuckles.

Kwan hurried to catch up. "It's about So-Young."

"So-Young?" I repeated.

"Has she ..." Kwan cleared his throat. "Has she talked to you about me?"

I stopped on the trail, hoping Kwan didn't see me blush. "I know that she considers you a dear friend."

"But has she ... spoken to you about her feelings? Romantic feelings?" Neither of us looked at the other. I spent the past several months trying to stifle my admiration for Kwan. So-Young loved him, even if she wouldn't admit that to me, and I wasn't about to come between her and the happiness she deserved.

"She hasn't mentioned anything specifically, but I know that she cares for you, even more than she wants to confess." I would rejoice to see So-Young happily betrothed, and there was no better match for her than Kwan. So why did my shoulders feel so heavy? "So-Young is a wonderful girl," I remarked, playing with a strand of hair so I didn't have to look at Kwan in the eye. "She will make a wonderful bride."

Kwan dug a hole in the dirt with the toe of his shoe. "I don't doubt that." After a long pause he added, "But not for me."

"What do you mean?" I glanced up for the first time since our conversation started. Kwan grabbed his finger but stopped before making the joint crack.

"I know that you and So-Young are dear friends. Even closer than sisters." I nodded, wondering if I should take off my sweater. Why had it felt so cold when we first started our walk? "That's why I have been so hesitant to talk with you." Kwan put his hand against a tree branch. I didn't realize until then that we both had stopped walking. "You see, Sister Chung-Cha ..." Kwan reached out and touched my trembling hand with his. "Although there has never been a spoken agreement between So-Young and me, I feel that I owe her an apology."

"An apology for what?" I didn't turn away as Kwan leaned his face down toward mine.

"An apology for falling in love with her best friend, instead of her."

ATTENDANT

"The friend who attends the bridegroom waits and listens for him, and is full of joy when he hears the bridegroom's voice. That joy is mine, and it is now complete." John 3:29

Kwan was already determined not to do anything in secret. The night of his confession, Kwan refused to talk to me again until he spoke with Mr. Kim about our relationship. I imagined Mr. Kim thought poorly enough of me and my tarnished past that he would forbid Kwan from courting me. Nevertheless, Kwan was adamant that he could persuade his employer and benefactor to allow our relationship to develop.

That evening when Mr. Kim came home, he and Kwan went outside to prepare the chicken coop for winter. As the two men headed outdoors, Kwan glanced over his shoulder at me and smiled. I looked at the floor, flushing even more deeply when I realized that So-Young was watching us both.

I hadn't seen my friend all day. She left early that morning to help a young mother care for her newborn son. So-Young sat in a small chair weaving. Sighing, I picked up the basket I started a few days earlier and lowered myself in the chair next to So-Young.

"Did you have a pleasant day?" she asked. My heart was too heavy for small talk, and my mind was too consumed with thoughts about the future. I barely heard her question. So-Young looked at me over her weaving and asked, "Are you feeling sick?"

"I don't know," I answered truthfully. I held my basket in my lap, but my hands remained idle. Usually I was relieved to have So-Young to talk to after a long and stressful day. Our conversations still make up some of my fondest memories from my time in Sanhe. There was only one subject So-Young and I never discussed together honestly.

"Did Kwan speak with you?" So-Young's fingers worked twice as fast as usual.

I wanted to hide my face. "How did you know?"

So-Young never put down her weaving, even as she gazed intently at me. "It was only a matter of time."

"What do you mean?" Was So-Young outside when Kwan and I were talking? Did she overhear our conversation?

"You and I are so close. We don't need to keep secrets any longer." So-Young's voice quivered, but only once. "I have not been honest with you about my feelings for Kwan because I didn't want your care for me to come in the way of your own happiness."

"That doesn't make sense. I was doing the same thing for you. I knew you loved him. You never told me, but I knew it anyway." So-Young looked out the window at the golden sunset. "I was afraid that Kwan might be developing feelings for me, so I did as much as I could to keep from encouraging him. The last thing in the world I wanted to do was to hurt you." Once again, I wondered why I didn't leave the safe house when Mrs. Cho offered me passage to her orphanage in South Korea.

"Kwan has never seen me as anything more than a child." So-Young smiled sadly at me over her weaving and sighed. "From the very beginning, I knew Kwan would love you."

"But how?"

So-Young shrugged. "Because I know Kwan as well as I know myself. When I met you, I knew that if you stayed here with us he would soon grow to adore you. Just as I have." It was So-Young's gentleness that made my heart ache, even more so than if she reacted in jealousy or anger.

My throat tightened. "I love you too much." I could never explain to So-Young everything I was feeling. "You deserve this joy. I could never take it from you." In my soul, I begged God to change Kwan's heart, to make him fall in love with So-Young instead of me.

So-Young took a deep breath. "Even if you were to walk out of the safe house tonight, even if you were to leave us and not return, Kwan would never look at me the way he looks at you."

I realized how unworthy I was of So-Young's friendship. "What do you think I should do?"

So-Young stopped her weaving and studied me. "Do you love Kwan?"

I ran my fingers through my hair. "I don't know. All this time, I imagined I was keeping myself out of the way so that you ..." I threw up my hands in confusion. I remembered Shin, the prison guard who helped me escape to China. Why did God bring me to Sanhe and let me ruin So-Young's happiness?

"You have a lot to think about." I wondered how So-Young, who was five years younger than I, could be so much wiser than I would ever hope to be.

"You're right."

"Kwan is a patient man," So-Young continued. "He'll wait until you're ready."

I realized with both envy and regret that So-Young would make a far more suitable wife for Kwan than I ever could.

"Why don't you get some sleep?" So-Young suggested. "Maybe you'll find your answers in the morning."

So-Young focused once more on her weaving. I crept into our room. When So-Young came to bed hours later, I closed my eyes and pretended to sleep. Instead I stayed awake listening to So-Young stifling her sobs as she buried her head in her pillow.

STRANGERS

"I am a stranger to my brothers, an alien to my own mother's sons." Psalm 69:8

Kwan and I were married the following summer. It was a quiet ceremony. So-Young helped me dress in a borrowed bridal jacket and skirt. As she tied the traditional knot around my waist, So-Young smiled.

"You are a beautiful bride." Over the past year, So-Young rejoiced with me as my love for Kwan blossomed. Today she played the role of the gracious and joyful bridal attendant, but in my heart I wondered how So-Young felt to see me in formal Korean wedding attire, preparing to marry the man she secretly loved for so many years.

Our wedding was attended by my safe-house family and Pastor Tong from Mr. Kim's house church. Mr. Kim stood in as a surrogate father of the bride, and I couldn't keep from wondering if he also would have preferred a different wife for Kwan on that day.

Kwan and I moved into one of the additions along the side of the safe house. In many respects, life went on as it did before our wedding, but I was surprised and disappointed that my marriage didn't bring the breathtaking bliss I imagined it would. I missed sharing a room with So-Young. My new husband was not much of a companion by the end of the day when he was weary from his long hours of labor and preferred to spend our time alone in wordless recreation, not in deep conversation. So-Young was often ministering in Sanhe from sun-up until sundown. Now that So-Young and I didn't spend our evenings together talking, I was plagued with overwhelming loneliness.

Even so, I knew that if So-Young and I had time for conversation, she wouldn't be able to understand my melancholy let down after my wedding ceremony. How could anyone who never experienced horrific abuse comprehend the fear and loathing I felt at my husband's touch? Neither could So-Young, who overflowed with selflessness and grace, understand the feelings of self-hatred that haunted me when I fought with Kwan. I spent over a year at the safe house spreading love and hope to any defector or abandoned baby who came to our door, yet when I was with my own husband I was overly critical, even rude and sarcastic.

Kwan was not the type of man who yelled at me in the heat of anger. When we argued, he had enough self-possession to keep his voice under control, but his words sometimes left gaping wounds in my spirit, wounds that So-Young would never be able to comprehend or heal. How I longed for someone more mature, someone like the Old Woman who was filled with wisdom and grace to help me during that tumultuous first year of my marriage. But Mr. Kim's rules kept me from venturing outside or forming relationships with others in Sanhe. Mr. Kim even forbade me from telling the defectors I met that I was from North Korea, just as they were.

Over the course of that first disheartening year, I lost my strength and my appetite altogether. I slept in so that more than once Mr. Kim accused me of being a drain on the safe house's scarce resources. It seemed an insurmountable task to pull myself out of bed to clean the chicken coop, make the morning meal, wash the dishes, then weave more baskets for the Kims to sell at the Sanhe market. I dreaded the days when defectors or other needy persons came to our door, instead longing only for sleep and solitude. The one person I knew to blame for my loneliness and gloom was Kwan, the man I should have turned to for comfort and support.

I tell you these things, beloved daughter, not to slander your father, but to give you an idea of what my life was like when I was a young bride. There were tears of bitterness and words of anger. There was hurt, and loneliness, and disappointment. But in many ways, the fault was my own. You see, I was never told before marrying that Kwan couldn't bring me complete satisfaction. Kwan was meant to be my companion and my supporter but never my idol. This is the lesson I failed to understand so many years ago, and the lesson I hope you will learn before you too become a bride. How I wish I could see you on that day ...

One of the biggest stresses on our marriage was my paralyzing fear of being discovered and sent back to North Korea. Although I was married to a Chinese citizen, in the eyes of both the Chinese and Korean governments, my marriage to Kwan meant nothing. To China, I remained an illegal immigrant, an unwanted societal parasite. The Chinese police despised me so much that they would pay eight hundred yuan to anybody who turned me in. To my homeland, I was a political and ideological traitor, deserving the highest forms of punishment fathomable if I was caught.

"If you're so scared, then why do you insist on remaining here in Sanhe?" This was a common argument between Kwan and me now, even a year after our wedding. The subject was bound to come up several times a week as I often complained that if I were free to move about the village then I wouldn't be so depressed.

"I already told you, I feel like God has called us here." Perhaps if my husband spent more time in prayer and less time scowling and fretting at night he might have discerned that I was right.

"If God has called you to stay here, then why do you brood all the time and whine about how hard it is?" Kwan kept his voice level, but his exasperation was unmistakable.

"I'm not God!" I clenched my fists. "I can't give an answer for him. Just because my life in Sanhe is hard or dangerous doesn't mean God doesn't want me here."

"If you are truly where God wants you to be, then you could at least try to be joyful," Kwan retorted. "What do you think it's like living with a wife who can barely pull herself out of bed and get her hair brushed in the morning before she needs to lie down and take a nap again?"

"This isn't about what you'd like!" I didn't care that Mr. Kim and So-Young were home and could probably hear me. Over the past year, I grew more and more certain that Mr. Kim regretted that Kwan married me instead of his daughter. I felt even more like an outcast in my safe-house family than I did before Kwan ever spoke to me about courtship or betrothal.

Kwan cracked his knuckles, making me grit my teeth. "Do whatever you want. It's not my responsibility to solve all your problems for you. I can't make you happy. That much is clear enough by now."

"Why do you always treat me like there's something wrong with me?" I tried to keep my voice at a reasonable volume. "I know you despise me, but why do you have to make it so obvious?"

"I don't despise you." Kwan rolled his eyes.

"Of course you do. You regret marrying a woman who grew up in a labor camp. You'd probably be happier if I were sent back to North Korea so you could forget all about me." I couldn't stop my words of hostility and accusation. "And if that's the case why don't you just turn me in to the police yourself? You'll get some money to spend and be rid of me at the same time."

Kwan stood up. His lower jaw twitched, and he stared at me with icy calmness. "I'm going on a walk." And because Kwan possessed Chinese citizenship ever since he immigrated to Jilin Province, and because he was therefore free to leave and enter the safe house whenever he wished, he went out without another word.

Shortly after Kwan left, So-Young knocked on the door to our room. I was sitting where Kwan left me, scowling at the dirt on our rug.

"Sister Chung-Cha?" So-Young whispered and opened the door. I didn't bother looking up at her.

"Come in," I muttered. The last thing I needed was So-Young's gentle and selfless nature to remind me that I was far from the refined, righteous daughter I was supposed to be.

"I wanted to let you know that my father will be gone for the evening." So-Young lowered her delicate frame onto my bed.

"More work on Pastor Tong's addition?"

So-Young shook her head. "An important meeting. House church leaders from all over eastern Jilin Province are gathering."

"What for?" Given the precarious situation between house churches and the government, such a meeting would be highly dangerous.

"The police have raided more churches than normal in the past months," So-Young told me. "Several pastors have been arrested. The ones that are left are meeting to discuss how to minister to the churches without leaders."

"I haven't heard anything about a meeting." I crossed my arms and stared at the tattered blanket on my bed, realizing how naïve I was one year ago when I imagined that by marrying Kwan I would become privy to the confidential inner workings of Mr. Kim's safe house. In fact, now that I was living in a separate room, cut off from the main living area, I knew even less about what was going on under the safe house roof than I did before my marriage. Mr. Kim never became the adoptive father-in-law I imagined he might. Sometimes Mr. Kim went weeks at a time without speaking to me at all. I missed the evenings So-Young and I spent together talking when we were both unmarried, sharing a single room together.

"Have there been any raids here in Sanhe?" I picked at a string from my blouse.

"Not in Sanhe, but in Longjing several pastors and evangelists have been arrested. The same thing has happened in Helong."

"Will Pastor Tong be safe?" I thought of the balding leader of Mr. Kim's home church. He and his pudgy adult son were the only citizens of Sanhe I would be able to recognize by sight.

"Pastor Tong's faced prison before. He's not afraid of another arrest."

"Who would lead the church in his place?"

"His son." So-Young folded her hands in her lap. "Or my father." I was grateful for So-Young and her friendship, but I also realized that it was Mr. Kim, her own father, whose stern dealings left me feeling more abased than a common household servant, and Kwan, the man she had grown up loving, who had just stomped out of my room after yet another argument.

I was about to ask So-Young about her day in the marketplace when she held up her finger.

"Did you hear something?" The noise returned. "It sounds like a baby." So-Young leapt to her feet and rushed to the front door. I was grateful that So-Young was home. I had no energy to care for anybody after such a trying evening.

"This child is burning with fever." So-Young picked up the infant and nearly threw him over her shoulder. She began to rub his back vigorously, but it did nothing to stop his coughing.

"Who would leave a child here in such a condition?" So-Young stood in the open doorway. "He doesn't need a nanny," she exclaimed. "He needs a nurse."

While I stood lamely by, So-Young grabbed a blanket. She wrapped it around the child as she rushed the croupy infant out the door toward the nurse's home.

I waited up, wondering if Kwan's mood would change. It didn't. When he returned, we exchanged chilled greetings, then Kwan sat by the fire. I retreated to our room, planning to pray for So-Young and the sick baby. Instead I spent most of the time complaining to God about my insensitive husband.

About an hour after the last rays of sun disappeared below the horizon, I was getting ready to go to bed without Kwan. Someone knocked vigorously on the safe-house door. I was in no mood to stay awake and minister to the needy, especially after my fight with Kwan, so I stayed in my bed and merely listened while Kwan opened the door.

"Please," a man said, "we need help. May we come in?" At his words, the hairs on my neck bristled.

"We've just crossed the Tumen River," a woman added. A forced tremor covered over the sickening sweetness of her voice. I got out of bed and peeked through my door at the strange couple who stood in the doorway.

"Please, come in." Ordinarily, I would have resented my husband for speaking kindly to strangers after dealing so wretchedly with me only a few hours earlier, but tonight I was consumed by darker and more menacing anxieties.

Kwan continued conversing with the strangers. I glanced around the room. What could I do to warn him? After thinking a moment, I picked up a glass pitcher that lay by the side of my bed. I held it high above my head and then smashed it on the floor. I let out a loud and deliberate shriek as the pieces crashed around my feet. A few seconds later Kwan rushed into the room.

"What happened?" He looked for a moment at the broken glass, glanced over at me, and then raised his eyebrows.

"Don't let them in," I whispered.

Kwan narrowed his dark eyes. "What are you doing, Wife?" I might have been afraid of his anger if I weren't so scared of the strangers outside my door.

"Just listen," I begged. "Those people are lying to you."

"Do you know them?"

I shook my head but remained silent. Shouting wouldn't prove my point.

"Is there a problem?" asked the man outside. "Perhaps my wife and I could be of assistance?"

"No!" I called out before Kwan could answer. "I cut my leg on some glass. Please, if you would wait outside for another moment, I'm not dressed decently. Please stay there."

"You're acting like a spoiled child," Kwan scolded. "Mr. Kim's policy at this home is to help anyone who is in need. Or maybe you have never bothered to read those verses in your father's precious Bible."

"If you knew who they were," I whispered back, ignoring Kwan's look of disgust, "you would send them away before they destroy us all."

"We've had a long journey," the woman called. "We were told you might help us."

"Don't come in!" I shouted. "I'm injured. If you want to help, you can go to the nurse's house. She lives near the school, along the road to Longjing."

"Longjing?" the woman snorted. "I saw no such road."

"Let's go," her partner ordered.

I shivered as the front door slammed shut. Kwan pinched me on the arm.

"I hope that you have an explanation for your behavior." Kwan dug his fingers into my flesh.

"They're guards!" I was frustrated that what was so obvious to me was not just as clear to my husband. "It's a trap, don't you see?"

"They just looked like a poor couple to me, the kind of couple that Mr. Kim established this safe house to help."

"Poor?" I shrieked, trying to keep my voice from hysteria. I wasn't as angry as I was terrified for my own safety. "Did you look at the woman? She nearly had a double chin!"

"Well, I ..."

"And the man!" I added. "Have you ever seen a refugee dressed like that?"

"But he ..."

"And since when are North Korean defectors familiar with any road that leads to Longjing?"

Kwan opened his mouth and forgot to shut it again. He rubbed his chin. "We'd better call Mr. Kim."

We didn't need to. As Kwan made his way to the phone, Mr. Kim barged into the safe house. "Is Chung-Cha safe?" Mr. Kim stomped to our bedroom and let out his breath when he saw me. He frowned at the broken water vase, but didn't ask any questions. "I just got word that an undercover raid is on its way."

"They were already here," Kwan muttered.

"What?" I never saw Mr. Kim so agitated before.

"They pretended they were defectors. Their disguise fooled me, but not my wife." Kwan's words might have made me feel proud were it not for the bitter sullenness in which he spoke them.

Whether Kwan was worried for my safety or brooding because I was correct about the strangers, I didn't have the chance to find out. At that moment Mr. Kim demanded, "Where is my daughter?"

FLIGHT

"Flee like a bird to your mountain. For look, the wicked bend their bows; they set their arrows against the strings to shoot from the shadows at the upright in heart." Psalm 11:1-2

I couldn't stop worrying about So-Young as I hurried beside my husband. Even though it was the middle of summer, I was shivering. "Are you cold?" Kwan asked me, holding my elbow as we rushed toward the mountain range between our hometown and Yanji.

Kwan carried a day's worth of provisions in a small bag. We started out two hours ago and just now approached the foot of the mountains. From behind a sheet of thin clouds, the crescent moon offered little light to our path. I leaned against a tree to steady my shaking limbs.

"We'll need to hurry to get to the cabin before daybreak," Kwan urged. "Can you wait until we start our ascent before we stop again to rest?"

I was out of breath. My legs threatened to collapse beneath me. If only Kwan understood. But I couldn't stop to explain things. We had to keep moving. I needed supernatural endurance, but God wasn't cooperating with my prayers.

Shortly after the visit from the two strangers, Mr. Kim decided Kwan and I had to flee. We were heading to the cabin of a former house-church leader who was hiding there from the Chinese police. Mr. Kim was the only person who had any contact with this religious exile, and he took several minutes to explain to Kwan the way to the cabin. Then Mr. Kim packed a small bag with some boiled eggs and cabbage rolls before pushing us out the back door.

Mr. Kim planned to stay at the safe house until his daughter returned, and then he and So-Young would follow us up the mountain. To stay safe, we had to assume my behavior in the bedroom would have alerted the undercover guards. I didn't know how much time Mr. Kim and So-Young had left. I was in the most danger since I would be sent back to North Korea if caught, but Kwan and Mr. Kim could also be arrested for helping refugees. I at least hoped So-Young would stay safe due to her age, but there was no guarantee for her protection either. Mr. Kim looked fragile and ragged when he prepared us for our journey. I was sure he was as worried about his daughter as I was.

Kwan and I walked as fast as we could all night long. About half an hour after the sun began to rise behind ominous storm clouds, we spotted a small structure in a clearing. "This must be it." Mr. Kim hadn't heard from his hermit friend in over a year and warned us that the cabin might be deserted.

Kwan knocked on a loose plank before entering. There was no door to speak of, only half a canvas hanging from a single nail. Kwan walked in first. The cabin was large enough to hold only a cot and a tree stump, probably intended for a chair. I was too exhausted from our mountain trek and too worried about our friends back in Sanhe to wonder about our supposed host.

"You can have the cot," Kwan offered. "I'll lie on the ground." It had been more than twenty-four hours since I last slept, but I knew I would be unable to rest until my mind slowed down.

"Do you think they've started on their journey yet?" I still couldn't find relief from my anxiety over So-Young's safety.

"They're probably only an hour or two behind us," Kwan assured me. He sat down on the floor. "With as many times as you needed to stop and rest, I'm surprised they weren't already here waiting for us when we arrived!" I knew he wasn't trying to hurt my feelings, but our recent fight and the threat of danger left my spirits too bruised for joking.

"I hope nothing happens to So-Young," I breathed into the semi-darkness. Kwan shifted over onto the little hammock and put his arm around me. Without thinking about it, I leaned into his wiry frame and rested my head on his chest.

Kwan leaned his cheek against my hair and took a deep breath. "I love you." I waited for him to apologize for the argument back at the safe house, but he just sat and let me absorb the strength and warmth from his body. In spite of our frequent conflicts, I was now terrified to think of being separated from my husband.

"Are you scared?" I could only nod in response. I waited for Kwan to lecture me, to remind me yet again that it would be best for us to immigrate to South Korea. "What if you have a child?" Kwan often mentioned. "How could we stand to raise a son or daughter in this sort of danger?" If only Kwan knew how his words resonated in my soul this morning, now that I tasted true danger for the first time since arriving in Sanhe. I waited for the lecture to resume anew, but after a short period of silence, Kwan patted my knee and stretched out again on the floor.

I tried to recline on the cot, but after a few minutes, I crawled to the ground beside Kwan. I thought through our argument at the safe house. Like so many other times, I had refused to go to South Korea, certain that God's work for me was in Sanhe. By my stubbornness, I put my family and our friends in danger. I couldn't shake the foreboding in my spirit when I thought about So-Young. When would the Kims be here?

And now I realized that I had another person to care about, another being whose life and safety were intricately connected to mine. A wave of protectiveness swept over me.

"Husband," I whispered as I wrapped my arms and legs around Kwan, as if I might hold on to him forever that way, "once we make sure So-Young is safe, let's go to South Korea."

RESCUER

*"Come quickly to my rescue; be my rock of refuge, a strong
fortress to save me." Psalm 31:2*

I woke up to the sound of driving rain. It was cloudy and
dark. There was no way to guess how long I slept. Kwan's coat
was wrapped around me, but it was soaked from the water
cascading in through the makeshift canvas door. Kwan was
hunched over on the tree stump next to me, holding his head in
his hands.

"Where's So-Young?" I was surprisingly alert for just
waking up.

"They haven't come," Kwan mumbled.

"What time is it?" I sat up and winced in pain. A nerve in my
back fired all the way down to my leg in protest.

"It's past noon."

"I thought you said they were only an hour or two behind
us." I wasn't trying to sound accusatory, but Kwan's face set
with characteristic defensiveness.

"How could I know the exact time that they left? Obviously I
can't be both here with you and back at the safe house at the
same time." I told myself that my husband wasn't angry with
me, just worried for our friends. I tried to lessen some of the
tension in the dark cabin.

"I just ... I ..."

Kwan rolled his eyes. How I wished he understood. I opened
my mouth but closed it again when Kwan stood up.

"I'm going to look for them," he declared as thunder
rumbled nearby.

"Right now? In this storm?" I wished I didn't sound so
irritated. "You must be crazy." But I knew there was no way to

change my husband's mind. Kwan wasn't an idle man. I couldn't expect him to wait here until the storm subsided, not knowing what had become of our friends. Willing away my tears, I held out Kwan's soaked coat.

"What good will that do me in this rain?"

"Please." If something happened to Kwan, I didn't want our last words to be angry. "Let's not keep fighting like this."

Kwan hardened his expression, shrugged his shoulders, and took his coat. He didn't even say good-bye as he left the cottage.

By nightfall, the storm clouds were gone. So was my husband. I had hoped Kwan would find Mr. Kim and So-Young on his way down the mountain trail and we would all be reunited in a few short hours. Kwan didn't leave me any directions to follow if he was delayed. I wasn't even sure I knew which path would take me back to Sanhe.

I wanted to pray. Desperately, I longed to pour my heart out to the Lord and find the comfort and assurance that only he can give. But along with my broken relationship with my husband came an obstructed communion with God. Often I tried to apologize to the Lord for my resentment toward Kwan, but usually my prayers did more to exonerate myself and slander my husband than to address the sinfulness that dwelt in my own heart.

I peeked into the bag of provisions that Mr. Kim sent with us. I ate a boiled egg for dinner, leaving one more egg and two cabbage rolls to last until whenever my husband returned.

If he returned.

During my first year of marriage, I often imagined Kwan's death. I hope that you do not think me a cold and unloving wife, but I must admit to you, beloved daughter, that I often pictured myself at Kwan's funeral, accepting the condolences of So-Young and Mr. Kim and Pastor Tong. In my mind, I always appeared so stately and composed. In the most distressing days of my turbulent marriage, I envisioned how many ways my life would be easier if I no longer had a husband. I could move into So-Young's room again and renew our late-night talks. Perhaps Mr. Kim would pity me as a widow and soften in his attitude toward me. Without the dark depression hanging over me – which I wouldn't be struggling with if Kwan were a better husband – I could be a much more competent servant for the Lord. I pictured myself ministering graciously and tirelessly as So-Young did, without the heaviness of spirit that dragged me down ever since Kwan and I joined our lives together.

But after a year of such thoughts, I realized that night how helpless I would be if Kwan died or was arrested, leaving me alone with minimal provisions on a completely unfamiliar mountainside. I sat shivering in the drafty cabin, mulling over all the horrific fates that might befall my husband as he searched for our missing friends. In addition to my anxiety for Kwan, I was convinced that something dreadful happened to So-Young. Why else hadn't Mr. Kim arrived here as planned? Although the storm clouds had vanished as quickly as they had appeared, leaving me closer to the stars than I had ever been, I could find no peace or solace.

When I woke up the following morning, Kwan was still missing. I waited in that dank cabin for three days. You might not believe, beloved daughter, how quickly I regressed to an almost primitive state of survival by the time Mr. Kim found me. At least once an hour during those days on the mountain, panic seized my body and allowed me only the shallowest gasps for air. With each spell, I was certain that I would die of suffocation. I sobbed uncontrollably, gasped the name of Jesus in a futile attempt to ward off the attack, and waited for death to end my suffering. But I always remained alive, left alone to wait for the next assault with little hope of reprieve.

On two different occasions I made up my mind to hike down the mountain, back in the direction I guessed was Sanhe. Twice I set off, but as soon as the cabin was out of sight, I started to hyperventilate, certain that if I took one step farther I would never find my way back to shelter. After the second failed attempt to leave my mountain abode, it took me half a day just to crawl back to the refuge of my deserted cabin home.

On the third night of being in such a wretched condition, I was lying on the cot and hoping that starvation might soon end my misery when Mr. Kim burst into the shelter. I cried out in terror when he entered the cabin.

"Be calm!" Mr. Kim ordered. I begged myself not to fall into another spell in front of Mr. Kim. He held out a boiled egg, already shelled. "You must be famished." Mr. Kim's voice was tense, without a trace of sympathy.

"Where's Kwan?" I questioned after I swallowed the last bite.

Mr. Kim looked at me through narrowed eyes and frowned. "We can't stay here any longer. It's time to move on."

"To Sanhe?" I noted with trepidation how much Mr. Kim had aged in the past four days.

Mr. Kim shook his gray head. "I'm taking you deeper into the interior. You'll be safer there." Mr. Kim winced as he said the words.

"Where is So-Young?" I was certain now that she would be here with her father unless something was wrong.

"Kidnapped." There was a terrifying lifelessness in Mr. Kim's eyes. "We don't know where she is." I didn't let the full weight of his words penetrate my heart just yet. There was something else I needed to know first.

"And Kwan?" I inquired, leaning against the cottage wall to steady myself as I stood up.

"Gather your belongings," Mr. Kim commanded. "We have a long journey. We need to start right away."

"And Kwan?" I repeated, strangely self-possessed. I lifted my head high and demanded again, "Where is my husband?"

Mr. Kim shuffled back and forth, his eyes not quite lifting to meet mine. He rubbed his cheek with a grubby finger, wincing as I stared at him.

"The police shot him." Mr. Kim walked out the doorway. "Your husband is dead."

TRAPPED

"Woe to me! The treacherous betray! With treachery the treacherous betray!" Isaiah 24:16

I followed Mr. Kim blindly. I was grateful that I didn't suffer another anxiety spell, but I couldn't understand why the news of Kwan and So-Young left me feeling nothing at all. Thinking that conversation might trigger some sort of reaction, I tried talking with Mr. Kim as we hiked further up the mountain.

"When did So-Young disappear?"

"The night that you left." Mr. Kim didn't offer any further comment.

"And the baby? The one she took to the nurse's?"

Mr. Kim just shrugged and grunted. I thought about So-Young, captured with a child under her care. Knowing my friend's compassion, I was certain that So-Young would do anything in her power to shield that baby. I refused to think about my previous experiences with guards and prayed that the grace and mercy that flowed from So-Young would somehow protect her from excessive violence and brutality.

Mr. Kim was even less helpful when I asked him about Kwan. "The police shot him." And so we traveled on in silence through the night. By the time we reached the mountain summit, I was dizzy with exhaustion.

"Please, I need to rest."

"No," Mr. Kim snarled. "Not here." And so we began to hike down the north-western slope.

Although I was weak and famished, I was too wary of Mr. Kim to ask him for something to eat. But after another hour of relentless descent I knew I would faint if Mr. Kim pressed me any further. Would I need to tell him?

"I'm sorry," I announced, "but I can't walk any farther." To make my point, I sat down and leaned against the trunk of a spruce. I was grateful that Mr. Kim didn't argue but only took turns glaring alternatively between my feet and his pocket watch.

"Where are we going?"

"That's not your concern." Mr. Kim slammed his pocket watch shut. "We're getting you to safety. That's what matters."

I didn't ask Mr. Kim any further questions.

"Get up," Mr. Kim commanded after another minute passed. "We can't be late."

I followed Mr. Kim's stooped frame in silence. What was Mr. Kim keeping from me? Did he still think that I would protest passage to South Korea after all that happened? Did he have a plan for me to escape but was afraid I would resist, even after losing my husband to the Chinese police? Was there more to Kwan's death that Mr. Kim hadn't told me?

It was just before dawn when we stopped at a spot where two mountain streams intersected. Without a word, Mr. Kim pulled out his pocket watch again. The pale moonlight revealed heavy beads of perspiration on Mr. Kim's forehead. He wiped his brow with the back of his hand. "They should be here by now," he muttered to himself.

"Who?"

A rustle behind some trees made me jump. Before I could react, two Chinese policemen forced their way onto the path in front of us. Each of them aimed a pistol at our heads.

Mr. Kim raised his hands high in the air, and I imitated him. Mr. Kim appeared calm. I tried to do the same. The guards spoke to Mr. Kim in Mandarin. He answered back with uncharacteristic obsequiousness. I kept trying to catch his eye, hoping to ascertain what they were talking about. One of the policemen pulled out an envelope. I wondered if somehow Mr. Kim had managed to bribe the police in exchange for my safety.

The policeman handed Mr. Kim a wad of bills, and his colleague grabbed my arms. I winced as he forced handcuffs on my wrists. Mr. Kim turned his face away from me. It was then I realized that I had just been sold.

"Don't!" I begged. "Please don't let them. You don't understand." Before the policemen dragged me away from Mr. Kim's side, I leaned over and whispered into my betrayer's ear, "I'm with child."

"I'm sorry." Mr. Kim hung his head low. "I did it to save my daughter."

PART FIVE

Chongjin,
North Hamyong Province
North Korea

INTERROGATION

"Sustain me according to your promise, and I will live; do not let my hopes be dashed." Psalm 119:116

"Name," the National Security agent demanded. I lost track of how many times I was interviewed in the past three weeks. First the Tumen Detention Center police with their barely decipherable Chinese accents questioned me, followed by the People's Safety Agency guards in Onsong after I was sent back to North Korea. Now I was being interrogated in Chongjin, North Hamyong after my transfer to the National Security Agency jail there.

"Song Chung-Cha." I stared at the North Korean officer's black army boots and remembered with pristine clarity the night of my family's arrest.

"Place of birth."

"Hasambong, North Hamyong Province."

"What were you doing across the border?"

I repeated the same answer I gave during all of my previous interrogations. "I was captured by a guard. He was defecting from his post at Camp 22 and forced me to go with him."

The three junior officers around the room laughed. "There's a story we haven't heard before!"

"I wonder how she paid him for her escape," another commented. "It certainly wasn't in yuan!" I tried to remain calm, but I was shaking. This was the first time I was questioned before such a large group. Each of the agents was heavily armed. I worried more for my unborn child than for myself. What would they do if they found out I was pregnant?

"I was forced to leave against my will," I insisted. It no longer mattered what was true and what was false. I lied so many times to my interrogators in the past three weeks that I no longer cared about something as nebulous as honesty. Things might have been different if I wasn't carrying Kwan's child in my womb, but now every ounce of maternal instinct I possessed demanded that I protect my baby. A blighted conscience seemed a small price to pay in exchange for my child's survival.

"What was the name and rank of this guard?" the officer wanted to know.

"His name was Shin. He worked in the detainment center at Camp 22 and then in the train depot. That's all I know."

"And what became of this guard of yours? This Shin?"

"He was shot and killed when we crossed the Tumen River." Memories of Shin's death left me numb. I hadn't even had the opportunity yet to process my own husband's murder. My only goal was to keep my baby alive throughout these endless sessions. "I was afraid to return to North Korea, and so I lived there in Sanhe."

"How long did you remain across the border?" The officer raised his eyebrow and glared at a clipboard, which probably contained my prison records.

He would know when I left Camp 22.

"A little over two years ago," I answered honestly.

One of the junior officers laughed. "A stupid peasant girl gets lost in a foreign country, and it takes her two full years just to find her way home!"

"It took her that long to realize that those Chinese are lousy lovers compared to the real men on this side of the boarder." The bawdy laughter in the room made me even more nervous than the thought of a harsh prison sentence. I put my hand on my abdomen.

"And did you have contact with anybody else in Jilin?" The officer ignored his comrades' vulgar comments and stared at my midsection with probing interest. I begged God to let me find mercy in his eyes.

"I stayed with a family there." I crossed my hands behind my back in an attempt to look more natural.

"Chinese or Korean?" the officer pressed.

"I don't know," I stated. The officer's eyes flashed.

"Answer my question, you pig!" He threw the clipboard onto the ground. I flinched when I heard it clank against the metallic leg of the desk. "Were they Korean, or were they Chinese?" the man demanded again.

"Both," I stammered. "They were Chinese citizens, but they were Korean by ethnicity. South Korean."

The tallest of the junior officers guffawed. "So they spoke Mandarin all day, then Korean when they were making love all night long."

"That's enough!" roared the interrogating officer, slamming his hand onto the desk so that it nearly toppled over. At his outburst I cringed, and the three junior officers stood up straight at attention.

"And did you have sex with anyone during those two years you were in China?"

The directness of the question shocked me. Blushing, I stammered a negative reply. I thought about the woman I met at the People's Safety Agency jail in Onsong, where I was first transferred from China. Obviously in the last stages of pregnancy, the woman was dragged out of her cell by guards and came back an hour later with two black eyes that stared at the world vacantly. Her abdomen was reduced to half of its previous size. She died that night after hemorrhaging all over the holding cell.

"You swear that no man in China had his way with you?" the officer inquired.

I shook my head.

Apparently unsatisfied by my answer, the man glared at one of his junior officers. "Get me a pregnancy test."

The room spun. If I had the power, I would kill before giving up the life within me. But how could I protect my baby against four armed men?

A guard thrust a plastic cup into my hand. One of the junior officers gawked at me with an open mouth. I looked questioningly at the interrogator.

"Pee in it," he snapped. I glanced at him and at the men surrounding me and realized that he expected me to do so right there in the middle of the room. My throat stung with the bitter taste of humiliation. I began to pull down the pants to my prison uniform when the officer bellowed to his subordinates, "Faces to the wall!"

I was surprised by this gesture of decency. Grumbling in protest, the three junior officers turned their backs to me. My interrogator stared at them, his teeth clenched so tight that the veins of his neck throbbed from underneath his collar. When I was finished, I handed him the cup. "Four minutes," he declared and dipped a plastic stick into it. "Four minutes to tell us if you are a lying whore."

The junior officers turned to face me again and passed the time by making more crude jokes. I was certain that the head officer was my only safety from their savage lusts.

The thought crossed my mind that the interrogating officer might offer me his protection in exchange for certain favors. I no longer had a husband, and I didn't expect God to intervene to save me. After all that I already endured, half an hour with this brusque stranger seemed a minimal price to pay for my child's welfare. I tried to catch his eye.

After a few minutes, the head officer cleared his throat. "You're not pregnant," he stated. I tried to conceal my surprise. The junior officers looked disappointed. I breathed a silent prayer of thanksgiving, but reminded God that my interrogation was still far from over.

BEHIND CLOSED DOORS

"...False prophets will appear and perform great signs and wonders to deceive, if possible, even the elect." Matthew 24:24

The interrogating officer walked in wide circles around me, his hands clasped behind his back. Each time his boots stomped on the floor, the picture of the Dear Leader that hung on the wall shook slightly.

"Your records show that you are a religious traitor," he said. I knew this subject would come up. My Christian past was the reason that I was transferred to the auspices of the National Security Agency, instead of being sentenced by the People's Safety Agency in Onsong like a common border crosser.

I survived the repeated questionings in Onsong without giving too many direct answers about my Christianity. Although I admitted to having a religious heritage, I was never forced to make a statement one way or the other regarding my current faith practices or beliefs. I knew that my time of questioning under the National Security Agency wouldn't be so lenient, and I didn't yet know how I would answer my interrogator.

"Did you have contact with Christians in Jilin?"

"No." This was an easy enough question, which I had already lied about several times.

"You didn't go to church? Talk with a missionary? Seek out a Christian safe house?"

"No."

The interrogator leaned close to me. "Then how did you find the family who sheltered you?"

I didn't have a ready answer. It was the cross on the door that identified the home as a safe house, but I couldn't mention this.

"The wife saw me hiding in a copse of thorn bushes," I stammered. "She said she would help me."

"What was her name?"

I made up some reply, certain that the pseudonym I just gave would be reported to the Sanhe police back in Jilin Province.

"And her family? Were they Christian?" The officer licked his upper lip, covered by coarse stubble.

"They weren't religious." I shrugged my shoulders in an attempt to appear unfazed.

The officer leaned so close to my face that I felt his prickly chin hairs against my cheek. "If it wasn't for sex and it wasn't for God, then why did they decide to help you?"

I was speechless. Why would any non-Christian risk life and personal safety to help an illegal immigrant? "I don't know." I flushed. The officer looked amused.

"Look at the Christian pig," he commented to his subordinates. "She doesn't even realize that her own Bible teaches her not to lie to governing members of the Party." He clucked his tongue at me.

"Tell us, Christian pig," he prodded, his voice dripping with scorn. "Do you believe in Jesus?"

"Yes," I replied, although my answer was more of a rebellious reaction to the interrogator's goading rather than a proclamation of true faith or boldness.

"She admits it!" the officer gasped in mock alarm. Then he turned to his junior guards and winked. "And you know how I like to have my way with these young Christian sows." The officers all laughed. "Now leave me," he ordered them. "I want to show this Christian slut what we do with her kind around here."

Still chuckling, the junior officers left the room. "Make sure you save some for us," one called behind his back.

"We'll be having some Christian pork for dinner tonight," another chuckled.

Once the door slammed shut, leaving me alone with the officer, I gritted my teeth together and held my breath, reminding myself that I could endure anything as long as my child remained safe.

"I know you're pregnant," the interrogator remarked. All the blood drained from my head, leaving me even dizzier, and I unclenched my fists. The officer held up the stick from the pregnancy test. "I just didn't want to give away our little secret." His smile was twisted, his voice saccharine.

Any pretense of boldness vanished. "Please, Sir," I begged, "I'll do anything. Whatever you ask. But promise that you won't hurt my child."

"Child!" the man spat. "What right do you have to bring a bastard brat into the world?"

"Please," I implored, "just tell me what you want me to do. Only let me keep my baby."

The officer stared at me, his forehead hardened with wrinkles. "Very well," he finally replied, spitting again on the ground. "You said you'll do anything?"

"Anything." I clenched my teeth and braced myself for whatever was to come.

"Tell me you are not a Christian."

"I am not a Christian." The words came out of my mouth with astonishing ease.

The officer glared at me, shaking his head. "You are a liar, and you are a coward." He yanked my arm and pulled me toward a closet door.

"What are you doing?" I gasped.

"Taking you away from here," the man snarled, his breath heating up my cheek, his fingernails digging into my flesh. "You're going back across the border. To safety."

DELIVERER

"No good tree bears bad fruit, nor does a bad tree bear good fruit. Each tree is recognized by its own fruit." Luke 6:43-44

We sped along in an armored National Security Agency van. I was dressed in the clothes of a wealthy Korean. The interrogating officer instructed me how to answer anyone who stopped us for questioning.

"Your name is Lee Hae-Won. You are my sister. Never married. You live in Musan and are visiting me for the week."

"And your name?"

"Just call me Brother," he snapped.

As we drove away from the jail, I tried to make sense of the past two hours. Brother – whoever he was – coerced me to renounce my faith, but he apparently planned in advance to rescue me. I glanced at the National Security agent out of the corner of my eye, trying to figure out what he really was. If he was taking me to safety as he claimed, his actions in the interrogation room were not only baffling, but unpardonable.

"Why so quiet?" Brother asked after we drove for some time. We were headed toward the Chinese border. No one stopped us for questioning.

I was quiet.

"Aren't you going to thank me for saving you?"

"Thank you," I mumbled. Regardless of who he was or what he did in the interrogation room, this man saved my child's life and perhaps even my own.

"It's not the gushing gratitude I would have expected."

I stared out of the van's windshield.

"Perhaps you're angry that your deliverer wears the uniform of a National Security agent?"

I remained silent.

"You want to ask me something," the officer pressed. "Don't you?"

Brother would continue to pester me until I gave in. "You are a ... a believer?"

"Would I be risking my life for you if I weren't?" Brother kept his eyes on the road ahead of us.

"Then why did you do it?"

"Do what?"

"Force me to deny my faith."

Brother shrugged. "Perhaps to show you what you're truly made of."

This officer's secrecy and uncanny composure were unsettling. Even if Brother was a Christian, how was I supposed to trust him? Either he was prone to vicious fits of rage and violence in spite of his faith, or he was such a convincing liar that I couldn't ever feel safe in his company.

"If I recall correctly," Brother defended himself, "I didn't force anything upon you. You begged for me to spare your child. Said you'd do *anything*." His voice rose to a sugary falsetto as he mimicked my pleas in the interrogation room.

"You left me no choice." I crossed my arms and turned my face away from my rescuer.

"It's a serious offense to deny the Savior," Brother chided.

It's a serious offense to force people to deny the Savior shot through my mind, but my teeth clenched shut before the inflammatory words escaped.

"'Anyone who loves his son or daughter more than me is not worthy of me,'" Brother continued. "Or am I misquoting that particular verse?"

Perhaps it was my own wounded pride, or the guard's familiarity with the Scriptures, that broke my brittle self-restraint. "And what about the passage that warns if anyone causes a believer to sin, he would be better off to have a millstone tied around his neck and be thrown into the sea?"

I wondered if I just signed my own death sentence, as well as my baby's. Brother only clucked his tongue. "You might want to find some less macabre verses to quote from time to time," he sighed with a shrug of his shoulders. "But at least now I know that the Bible I gave your father when you were barely toddling was put to some use."

I nearly gagged on my own retort. The Korean officer turned in his seat and grinned at me. Still managing to keep his eyes partially on the road, he tipped his head in a feigned bow.

"Brother Moses," he announced. "Your humble servant."

UNVEILING

*"Like one from whom men hide their faces he was despised, and
we esteemed him not." Isaiah 53:3*

"Moses?" I could scarcely utter the name, which had been so
sacred in my childhood memories.

"You've heard of me, I see."

I felt nauseous. "You're a guard?"

"If you're talking about the uniform, I admit the color doesn't
suit me." Moses' lip turned upward in a lopsided grin.
"Nevertheless, I find this shade of green much more flattering than
that olive color they wear across the border. Wouldn't you agree?"

"But ... you're Korean," I somehow managed to stammer. "I
always thought you were Chinese."

Moses shrugged. "I left my Chinese passport at home today."

"But even the Chinese think you're one of them!"

"Do they?" Moses gasped. "I hadn't heard. Is there anything
else I should know about myself?"

It seemed impossible that this coarse, sarcastic officer was
the same hero I once venerated.

"Did Father know?"

"Know what? That I'm a guard? Of course not," Moses
declared. "I'm no fool."

"Then what exactly are you?"

Moses chuckled. "I'll allow you to answer your own
question. Who would you say that I am?"

The strain of my betrayal, capture, and interrogation left me
very little patience. I wasn't about to give this charlatan more
respect than he deserved. "I would say that you are a brutal,
violent killer who wears the clothing of a wolf, yet calls himself a
sheep," I replied, without either forethought or fear of retribution.

Moses clucked his tongue. "You forget that it was I who saved you," he replied. "What wrong have I committed against you, righteous daughter, to deserve such wrath?"

"You wear the uniform of the enemy. That in itself is enough. And you also tricked me. I would never have denied my faith if I knew who you really were. Your deceitfulness is the worse hypocrisy of all."

"Hypocrisy?" Moses asked and then suddenly grew quiet. "Yes, I suppose I am a hypocrite," he mused, "in that my comrades know nothing of my work for the underground church."

"Nor would they suspect it," I mumbled.

"You are referring to my coarse manners? I imagine I don't come across quite as holy and righteous as you probably pictured me. I'd like to see you survive five minutes as a National Security agent without growing even more cynical and contemptuous than the guard who just risked his life to rescue you. I don't have the luxury to be refined and sanctified like you."

"Which makes you both a hypocrite and a liar." Why had I venerated this impostor when I was a child?

"Well, then, I'm sorry if I am not everything you imagined I would be." I wasn't sure if this was also part of Moses' charade, so I moped for several minutes in silence.

"You think I'm a boor," Moses finally stated. I didn't deny it. "You should pity me instead."

"And why should I pity you?"

Moses ignored my challenge. "Tell me. You were married in Jilin, were you not?"

I raised my head high. "Yes, I was."

"And is your husband a righteous, God-fearing man?"

"He was until he was killed by the police."

Moses raised an eyebrow at me, then flicked his wrist in my direction. "And did this righteous husband of yours make sacrifices for the Lord?"

"More than you could imagine," I answered, immediately forgetting all of Kwan's shortcomings that seemed so unbearable to live with while he was still alive.

"Tell me," Moses pressed, "do you believe your husband will be rewarded in heaven for these sacrifices?"

"Yes." I straightened up in my seat. "I'm sure of it."

"Good." Moses snapped his finger. "Thank you. You have given me much hope."

"What do you mean?" I was weary of this agent's impudence.

"You see," Moses explained, "I also make sacrifices for the Lord, sacrifices that many good, upstanding Christian men would not be capable of making."

"Such as?"

"Such as knowing that fellow Christians are terrified of me," Moses answered. "Knowing that if they realized who I really was, they would tell me I was wrong to work for the National Security Agency."

"So you're defending yourself?"

"If I were not an officer, where would you be right now?" Moses contested. "And what would become of your child?"

I had no answer to give him.

"My position of authority allows me to save dozens of lives a year. And you – you, whom I just delivered – would tell me I'm sinning to keep up my work? I thought Hyun-Ki's daughter would have more wisdom than that."

I tried to think of an intelligent reply. "Surely there must be another way."

"If you tell me what it is," Moses stated with a wave of his hand, "I'll happily announce my resignation to the head of the National Security Agency this very night."

"But the cruelty, the torture ... I'm sure you can't save everyone there!"

"That's why you should pity me." Moses remarked, lowering his voice. I didn't want to think about the implications of his words.

"Then why don't you quit?"

"Because if I stopped working as a guard, the child in your womb would be dead by now. And so might you." Again I had no counter to Moses' arguments. I thought about the woman who bled to death in the Onsong jail.

"Some people would call me a coward," Moses went on, "because I do not live out my faith openly like your father did. They don't realize that if I confessed my love for Christ when I was first saved as a young guard, I would be dead. And so would the hundreds of Christians I've helped rescue over the past two decades."

"But couldn't God have used you in some other way?" As soon as I voiced the question, I realized how naïve it would sound to someone like Moses.

"It's not what you typically think of as mission work." Moses stared through the windshield at the road ahead of us. "Even now, I don't know if my life has done more to further the kingdom of light or the kingdom of darkness. It is God alone who must decide that."

We drove on in silence.

"The truth about my identity is not common knowledge," Moses admitted after some time. "I don't make it a habit to transport prisoners myself."

"Then why am I here?" I asked. "And why did you tell me who you are?"

Moses cleared his throat. "For nearly twelve years, I've lived with the regret that I didn't act in time to save your father. Every day I hoped you might find a way to escape Camp 22. First I saw the report that said you perished in a fire in the train depot, then I received word from Mr. Kim that you were under his care."

"You know Mr. Kim?"

"I know Mr. Kim," Moses replied. "I also know your husband Kwan."

I was surprised that Moses was so familiar with my safe-house family from Sanhe. "How?"

Moses shook his head. "There are many things I can't tell you." As if hearing my unspoken question, Moses added, "Like most believers, your friends think that I am a Chinese citizen. They have no idea what I really am." The loneliness in Moses' voice was unmistakable.

"So you have been looking out for my protection?"

"More than you would know," Moses answered. "I owed your father many debts of kindness. As I already told you, one of my deepest regrets is that I couldn't help him before his death."

"But your jurisdiction is over Chongjin. What could you possibly have done for him in Camp 22?"

Moses furrowed his brow. "Camp 22?"

"Where they took Father after he was shot at the precinct building." I wondered why Moses, who appeared so familiar with every other aspect of my family history, now looked so confused.

"I've seen the death record myself," Moses replied. "Your father died in Hasambong."

I didn't understand. "That's not true," I insisted. "Father died in detainment. He …" I stopped, unable to speak to Moses of Father's suicide.

"Sister," Moses said, with a gentleness I wouldn't have thought possible beforehand, "I can only imagine what your guards must have told you when you were a young girl." I remembered my torturer Agent Lee, his sarcastic laugh, his gleeful expression when he told me of Father's hanging. "If I knew," Moses continued, "I assure you that I would have done everything in my power to dispel their lies many, many years ago."

"What are you saying?" My head was faint again.

Moses took a deep breath. "Hyun-Ki was killed by a bullet the night your family was arrested."

I put my hand up to my head to try to control the spinning. Moses reached out and touched my shoulder. "Your father was never a prisoner at Camp 22."

REVELATION

"Then you will know the truth, and the truth will set you free."
John 8:32

For several minutes, I could scarcely breathe, let alone speak. The weight of Moses' words was crushing. Perhaps, beloved daughter, you would expect me to rejoice that my father's memory was no longer tarnished by his alleged apostasy and suicide. But joy was not my initial reaction when Moses told me the truth about Father's fate. Instead, I had to face the horrific realization that everything in my past – my heart hardening against the Lord, my decision to become an office maid, my inability years later to fully trust in God's goodness – was based on a lie. Perhaps this was what my torturer intended all along.

Beloved daughter, how I wish that you and I had more time together so that your memories of me would be of joy and lightness and merriment. I imagine that when you read my story, you will come to know me as a wounded, pitiful character from your distant past, instead of the laughing, gentle mother I hoped to be for you. But truth can't be changed. My life has been filled with much sadness, and I've shed many tears. But never do I remember crying as I did beside Moses in that van. I cried for the innocence I lost in the detainment center, for the shame I carried around in my young soul about my father's supposed fate. I cried for my own rebellious heart, for my unwillingness to trust in God's sovereignty when the Almighty had indeed sustained Father and gave him boldness to his dying breath.

Moses drove on in silence. By the time the Tumen River came into view, my throat was sore from sobbing, but my tears had run dry.

"They say that truth will set you free." Moses referenced one of Father's favorite verses. I nodded. "And now that I have told you the truth about your father," Moses added with uncharacteristic humility, "I wonder if you would repay this unhappy guard. You see, you have some important information that I've been seeking for years."

I wondered what I might know that Moses couldn't learn from my prison records. I waited curiously.

Moses rubbed the coarse hair on his chin. "I must confess something to you. The respect I harbor for your father and the many debts of kindness I owe him were not the only reasons I chose to rescue you from the Chongjin jail."

"They weren't?"

Moses shook his head. "I also revealed myself to you because I hoped that you could tell me about my mother."

I wondered how Moses expected me to understand his words. "Your mother?"

"Before she died, my mother was a prisoner in the underground detainment center at Camp 22." Moses exhaled loudly. "Your records show that you were her cellmate for nearly a year."

"You are Chul-Moo?" I asked when I realized that I was talking to the Old Woman's eldest son. Moses winced at the mention of his birth name.

"I see that she told you about me," Moses replied, and for the first time since I met him, the prison guard slouched down in his seat. I did not know what to say to the officer who was responsible for the annulment of his parents' marriage, the murder of his younger brother, and the twenty-four-year detainment of his mother in an underground torture cell. Then I remembered the Old Woman's words: *"I am not the Lord God Almighty; I do not pretend to know his plans for Chul-Moo, which may yet be for good."*

Moses watched me intently. "Can you please tell me if my mother ever forgave me for what I did to her? For what I did to our family?"

I couldn't help but smile when I remembered the grace and gentleness that flowed from the Old Woman. "Your mother was incapable of bitterness. She was heartbroken, I believe, but even in her sorrow she recognized that God might still take hold of your life."

"That he did." Moses had a distracted look in his eyes. I wanted to ask Moses how he became a Christian after condemning his entire family to labor camp, but he just stared ahead, talking as if to himself.

"I have witnessed countless atrocities against mankind. Each and every time, I tell myself that I am doing the only thing I know how to do, that the Almighty must see that my efforts are to serve him even if I am incapable of saving everybody." I didn't have the wisdom to either confirm or assuage the guilt on Moses' conscience. "But the one thing I haven't been able to forgive myself for is what happened to my mother. And my brother."

"Your mother was full of grace and gentleness." And as we continued to drive along the Tumen riverbank, I told Moses about my time in the Old Woman's cell, about the miraculous healing she performed for Shin's daughter, about the way I was healed from my deadly fever when I first met her. Moses was relieved when I told him of the privileged treatment his mother received in detainment and shocked to learn about her foiled execution so many years ago, which was never recorded in the Old Woman's prison record.

Moses asked several questions, which I tried to answer. Thankfully I never had to tell Moses what happened to his mother's body after she died. By the time our conversation ran its complete course, it was almost evening. We drove on in silence. I still didn't know how Moses planned to get me across the patrolled border. When the sun was low on the horizon, Moses maneuvered the van and parked it a short way from the bridge that crossed the Tumen River into Jilin Province, China.

"What are you doing?" I asked.

"Exactly what my namesake did in the Bible." Moses grinned as he glanced at my midsection. "Leading a captive people to freedom."

WATCHMAN

"I have made you a watchman for the house of Israel; so hear the word I speak and give them warning from me." Ezekiel 33:7

Staring wide-eyed at the border patrolman stationed on the middle of the bridge, I waited for Moses to explain how I was to cross the border. After a long period of silence in the parked van, Moses reclined in the driver's seat and stretched out his legs. "Your escort will be arriving soon," he announced. I was about to ask for more information when Moses turned toward me. "I hope that you don't despise me for my position." He held my gaze with unwavering eyes.

"No," I insisted, but I knew it would be difficult to sort out how I really felt about Moses and his work for the National Security Agency.

"It's a lonely life," Moses explained. "Perhaps that's another reason why I chose to rescue you personally. I wanted someone to know who I was." Moses rubbed the palm of his hand against his stubbly chin. "In case something happens to me one day." I grimaced when I recognized the resignation in Moses' voice.

"Aren't there others who know who you are?"

"No one but you," Moses admitted. "At least ... no one who remains alive today."

I couldn't fathom why Moses entrusted me with such weighty knowledge. It was a burden I didn't want to bear. "Why me?" I inquired.

Moses paused, staring up toward the ceiling of the van before he spoke. "No one at the Chongjin jail would even suspect the truth about my identity." Remembering Moses' mannerisms during the interrogation, his admission didn't surprise me. "And although I know of a handful of sympathizers within the National Security Agency, even they don't know that I'm on their side." Moses flinched, and I found myself wondering how many prisoners this officer was forced to condemn in his role as a National Security agent.

"As head official of the Chongjin jail, I've had access to classified reports. In addition, I have 'accidentally' discovered certain memos from Pyongyang, information that not even my superiors are supposed to know. There's no doubt you've suffered much, but even you wouldn't believe me if I were to tell you of all the atrocities that our government carries out against its own citizens. What you experienced in the labor camp was not even a fraction of the cruelty that our vile nation inflicts upon its own people."

I wanted to cover my ears. Could anyone suffer more than I had?

"If I were to defect now," Moses explained, "they would search for me from one end of the globe to the other. I have seen too much. I know too much. I will never be free." I couldn't guess how Moses had come to possess such nationally-incriminating intelligence, but I couldn't argue with the haunted expression in Moses' eyes.

"And so I am relying on you to be my mouthpiece of truth," Moses declared. I sat up rigid in my seat in the van. "You must tell the outside world what is happening behind these closed borders."

"But there are hundreds of defectors," I protested. "And some of them were guards and officers themselves," I added, remembering my guardian Shin. "What could I tell others that they haven't already heard?"

"Tell them that the state of North Korea as we know it is going to collapse." I clenched my jaw at Moses' fateful proclamation. "There's already such instability that the end will probably come soon."

Once again I wished I could close my ears to such prophetic utterances and blind my eyes to Moses' fiery black stare, but he wouldn't release my gaze.

"What do you want me to do?" My voice was nothing more than a pitiful squeak.

"You must tell believers on the outside to prepare for the day when the prison walls that surround our nation finally collapse. There will be a flood of refugees who will require both practical and spiritual care. The body of Christ in both China and South Korea must be prepared to minister to the needs of these exiles." Moses didn't pause for breath. "Within these borders, there will be a need for a concerted missionary effort unseen in recent history. We will need Bibles, missionaries, relief workers, doctors, humanitarians. And if the global church doesn't start preparing now, they won't be ready when the time comes."

"I'll tell them," I whispered, even though I didn't know how I would even begin such a daunting task.

"Promise me."

"I promise." I hoped that Moses couldn't detect the uncertainty in my voice.

HOMECOMING

"See, I will bring them from the land of the north and gather them from the ends of the earth. Among them will be the blind and the lame, expectant mothers and women in labor; a great throng will return." Jeremiah 31:8

Before Moses could say anything more, a high-pitched buzz sounded from his coat pocket.

"What's that?" I asked.

"The signal."

"What signal?"

Moses smiled and shrugged his shoulders, his mood reverting again from deadly serious to flippant and cavalier. "I'm escorting you across the bridge."

"You can't just drive me across the border!" I protested.

"I can if you have this." Moses tossed a Chinese passport into my lap. I opened it and saw a picture of an unsmiling Korean girl.

"What does it say?" I asked, squinting as I tried to read the small script.

Moses looked at the passport over my shoulder. "'Song Chung-Cha,'" he read, "'Chinese citizen. Jilin Province.' Down here is where your date of birth is recorded. Did you know that you were born in Seoul? Your family immigrated to China when you were a baby."

"How did you ..." I started to ask, but Moses interrupted me.

"The picture is the closest representation I could find without having met you personally. I'm sorry to say that it doesn't come close to capturing your beauty, but it will certainly serve its purpose. You will also need this." Moses handed me a small yellow card.

"A residency paper?" I remembered So-Young's identification card that I took with me whenever I went walking outside with Kwan. It seemed so long ago when my betrothed and I enjoyed our evening strolls together through the forest behind the safe house.

"It says you are a legal resident of Sanhe, Jilin Province. Hold on to it carefully. I don't want to see you on this side of the border ever again." Moses' voice was firm, but he winked at me playfully.

"These documents must have been expensive."

Moses flicked his wrist as if to wave my comment away. "I wasn't the one who paid for them."

"Then who did?"

"A citizen of Sanhe. A certain man you know as Mr. Kim."

For three weeks, I tried to make sense of Mr. Kim's betrayal. "Was that part of the plan all along?" I finally asked, figuring there were hundreds of less dangerous ways to get me proper identification.

Moses shook his head. "No. What Mr. Kim did to you was a grievous mistake, but perhaps the Lord ordained it so that you would have these." Moses tapped my passport and residency paper. "Mr. Kim used the bribe money he received from the Jilin police to purchase your documents, although that was not his original intention."

"He said he did it for So-Young." I didn't bother to ask how Moses had so much contact with Mr. Kim when he worked full time in the Chongjin jail.

"A father will do nearly anything for his child," Moses observed. "So will a mother."

I didn't want to think about my own test in the interrogation room or how quickly I faltered when I imagined my child was in danger. "Do you know what became of So-Young?" The only solace I found over the past three weeks since my betrayal was the hope that Mr. Kim's actions indeed saved my friend. When Moses shook his head, I sighed and stared at the Tumen River.

"Are you ready?" Moses turned the key to start the van and drove slowly toward the bridge. I tried to ask Moses what was going to happen, but I couldn't find my voice. I held my breath as Moses rolled the van toward the customs office that stood in the middle of the bridge and hoped that my deliverer had a plan for my safe crossing. A Chinese border guard scurried out to meet us and bowed to Moses.

"Can I help you?" he offered in Korean, eyeing me curiously.

"You'd better hope so!" Moses roared, his face growing red. "This woman, cousin by marriage to the mayor of Sanhe, was deported to my jail in Chongjin. Although South Korean by birth, she is a citizen of Jilin Province, but apparently she was so frightened during a surprise raid by your barbaric police that she didn't understand the questions those animals were shouting at her. They assumed she was a defector and sent her to my jail, yet here is her residency paper and even a passport. I would like to know how she got so far into our country without this mistake being discovered."

The guard lowered his head. "I am exceedingly sorry, Sir," he exclaimed, careful not to address me directly.

"I hope that whoever is responsible for this grievous error decides to stay away from her cousin the mayor for quite some time."

"Certainly. My deepest regrets." The man bowed again as if he himself were to blame for the alleged mistake.

"I am also convinced that you will see fit to offer this young woman safe passage back to her home without any further delays."

"Of course," the guard stammered. "I will escort her myself over the bridge. Do you wish for me to arrange a car to take her to her home in Sanhe?"

"I wouldn't entrust her to your care for a thousand yuan," Moses retorted, the blue veins in his neck throbbing from beneath his officer's collar. "I have already sent word to her brother. He is probably waiting for her on the other side of this bridge. If you have any sense, you will not make her brother angry. I'm also certain that you will compensate him for his trouble coming all the way out here to pick up his sister after such a horrendous display of your nation's incompetency."

"We will arrange all the details," the Chinese guard assured Moses. "Whenever the young lady is ready, I will drive her across in my van."

"Good. Good-bye, Miss," he bid me formally. I realized that there would be no chance for me to thank Moses for his rescue or to say good-bye. I wondered if I would ever see Moses again. "My sincerest apologies for the misunderstanding."

I hoped that the guard wouldn't try to speak to me in Mandarin as he helped me into his van. He apologized several times in Korean as we drove to the Chinese side of the border. "Is this your brother?" the guard asked once we stopped.

I looked out the window and there, pacing in front of a parked car and cracking his knuckles, was my husband Kwan, looking angry and nervous, but very much alive.

REDEEMED

*"O Israel, put your hope in the LORD, for with the LORD is
unfailing love and with him is full redemption. He himself will
redeem Israel from all their sins." Psalm 130:7-8*

"Sister!" Kwan greeted. I didn't have to feign my relief as he
hugged me. The officer spoke with my husband in Mandarin and
handed him a large sum of money, all the while continuing to
bow obsequiously toward us both.

Once we were alone in the car driving toward Sanhe I turned
to my husband. "I thought you were dead!"

"Dead?" Kwan's eyes opened wide before narrowing in
anger. "So he told you I was dead? That fool of a traitor!"

"Mr. Kim?"

"Who else? The same man who sold you for eight hundred
yuan while I was out risking my life to save his daughter."

"So you weren't shot?"

"No."

"Arrested?"

Kwan snorted. "Not quite."

"What happened then?" I asked.

"So-Young was kidnapped on the way to the nurse's."

"By whom? The police?"

"No. Mr. Kim never allowed me to tell you, but he and So-
Young are not really from Seoul. They are from South
Hwanghae Province, North Korea. After they arrived in Sanhe,
Mr. Kim had their papers changed to show Chinese residency
and citizenship."

"So-Young never told me."

"That's because she didn't know," Kwan remarked. "She
was very young when they came across the border. She

suffered much in her homeland and doesn't remember anything from her time in North Korea." I thought of my friend, so gentle and so mature. I wondered how much she endured before finally escaping to Jilin Province.

"What does this have to do with the kidnapping?"

"Someone found out the Kims were in Sanhe illegally. It was all a trap, even the sick baby. They caught So-Young on the way to the nurse's, then sent word to Mr. Kim demanding ransom money." I thought about my four days alone in the deserted cabin on the mountainside, when I was so anxious over So-Young's safety.

"Is that what compelled Mr. Kim to turn me in?"

In the passenger seat beside my husband, I winced as Kwan maneuvered the steering wheel with one hand and tugged on his knuckles with the other. "I went out to negotiate with So-Young's captors. I couldn't return to you earlier because the safe house was being watched. Mr. Kim was supposed to go to the cabin and bring you more food and tell you to wait a few more days. I never suspected he would do something as spineless and cowardly as sell you to the police for bribe money."

"Is So-Young safe now?"

"She was already safe before Mr. Kim returned from betraying you on the mountaintop. I told the brutes responsible for the kidnapping that we would leave the region and give them the title to the safe house. We were all going to leave for South Korea. The plan would have worked out wonderfully. You, me, Mr. Kim, and So-Young ... we could have all been in Seoul by now if it weren't for that dog's greedy, underhanded treachery."

"But now everybody is out of harm's way?" I pressed, clutching Kwan's forearm.

"They didn't hurt So-Young, if that's what you're anxious about. She and her coward of a father are already in South

Korea. They wanted me to come along as well, but I said that I would wait here for you, even if the kidnappers took over the house, and I had to live out on the streets."

I never remember feeling so much respect and admiration for my husband. "But why would Mr. Kim tell me you were dead?" I wondered.

"Perhaps he imagined he was being merciful to you." Kwan spat out his open window. "Maybe he thought if you believed that your husband was dead, it would make it easier to face all that abuse and torture he sold you into. It makes no sense to me."

"He was thinking about So-Young. Parents will do many things for the children they love." I wished that I could tell Kwan about the officer who rescued me, but I didn't know if even that was safe. There were so many questions I didn't ask Moses, so many things we didn't have time to discuss. "You know that Mr. Kim ended up using the ransom money to buy me a Chinese passport and residency papers, don't you?" I asked my husband.

Kwan shrugged. "If he hadn't sold you, he wouldn't have needed to. He was lucky that Mo ..." My husband stopped himself mid-sentence and rubbed his cheek. "He was lucky that he knew someone who could help."

Kwan was silent. I tried to think of something to say to lift his spirits. "I've never seen you drive a car," I remarked, trying to sound light-hearted. "It suits you well."

"I wouldn't have had to drive it all the way out here if it weren't ..." Kwan's voice drifted off, and he glared at the winding road.

"At least now we can go to South Korea directly since I have a valid passport." Kwan clenched his jaw and said nothing. "After all," I added, touching my husband's hand, "our baby will need to grow up in a safe place, away from all the guards and police and surprise raids."

Kwan turned to look at me until I was certain he was about to drive the car off the road. "Baby?" Kwan swerved at the last minute to straighten out the vehicle before it hit a tree.

I smiled at my husband, basking in his open admiration and surprise. As we drove back to Sanhe, my heart was filled with more hope than I thought possible when I woke up that morning a prisoner in the Onsong jail.

PART SIX

Seoul
South Korea

CALLED

"When you are old you will stretch out your hands, and someone else will dress you and lead you where you do not want to go."
John 21:18

I smiled in spite of my exhaustion as the chubby toddler tickled my belly. My back ached, and my ankles were so swollen my shoes didn't fit anymore. It was a miracle I could even walk.

"Baby! Baby! Wake up, Baby!" the almost three-year-old sang and blew a kiss on my abdomen. Since there was no longer any room for sitting on my lap, the girl from Mrs. Cho's South-Korean orphanage cuddled next to me on the couch.

"Auntie Chung-Cha?" asked her twin, pulling my arm. She was the more vocal of the two sisters, and much more serious as well. "When can I hold your baby?"

"Not yet." I stroked her jet black hair. It was just long enough for me to tie up in two short pig tails. "You have to wait until Baby is born."

Mrs. Cho entered the room, and the girls stopped touching my belly. "Look at these pillows." Mrs. Cho shook her head. She clucked her tongue at the girls and suppressed a grin. "You pick them up right now." The twins jumped off the couch to obey, but as soon as the pillows were in their proper places, the sisters cuddled next to me once more, rubbing my abdomen whenever Mrs. Cho happened to look away.

"Can I help you with anything?" I offered my benefactress, earning my own glare of disapproval from Mrs. Cho. Since I arrived at her home in Seoul nearly five months earlier, the orphanage matron refused to let me assist her in any household work. My days were filled resting and playing with the orphans for as long as my limited energy would allow. "You need practice with children," Mrs. Cho often reminded me with a grandmotherly smile.

"Auntie! Auntie!" The little girl's pigtails bobbed up and down as she tried to get my attention. "Why isn't Uncle home?" She pouted.

"Uncle Kwan had to go away. He'll be back soon." I tried to sound cheerful, but I don't think I succeeded. Mrs. Cho came up behind me and rubbed my shoulders.

"Come out now, Baby!" her sister commanded to my midsection, raising her voice and pursing her lips together. She put her hands on her hips.

"The baby isn't ready to come out yet," the pigtailed twin scolded, then turned to me as Mrs. Cho repositioned a barrette in her hair. "Will Uncle Kwan be home when Baby's born?"

"Hopefully," I sighed, although with each passing day and each contraction of false labor, it became harder and harder to hold on to hope.

***

Kwan returned to China thirteen days after we arrived at Mrs. Cho's orphanage in Seoul. Those two weeks we spent together brought with them the sweetness of new marriage that we could never find for ourselves in Sanhe. It probably didn't hurt that we had spent the past three weeks separated, convinced we would never be together again. In Seoul, safe from the threat of raids and repatriation, Kwan and I did very little but talk and dream together about the child we conceived.

"He'll be strong," Kwan told me. "Like your father."

"Perhaps it's a girl."

"Then she'll be beautiful," Kwan declared, "like you."

Unfortunately, the bliss Kwan and I experienced once we were finally safe in South Korea was short-lived.

"Pastor Tong was arrested again," my husband told me only a week and a half after we arrived in Seoul.

I was frightened by the determined look etched in Kwan's face. "Is it a harsh sentence?"

"Life." When Kwan wrapped his arm around me, I realized I was trembling.

"Who's left to care for the church?"

"Mr. Kim is already here in South Korea." Kwan cracked his knuckles. "Not that I would trust that double-crossing dog to offer spiritual care to anyone."

"So who does that leave back in Sanhe?" I wondered why this news sent chills up my spine.

"That pastor's son." Kwan sat on our bed next to me. "He's now the only one." Kwan stared at me for so long I finally looked down at the floor.

"I'm going back," he announced, in that instant curtailing whatever honeymoon period we enjoyed.

Kwan stood up. "I'll do everything in my power to return before autumn." That promise was made nearly five months ago. Sitting on Mrs. Cho's couch beside the two twins, I watched out the window while some of the older children played outside in the snow. I leaned my cheek against one of the girl's head and thought about the last time I saw my husband. He came into our room just moments before his cab was scheduled to take him to the airport.

"I'll be back soon." Kwan brushed a stray strand of my hair behind my ear. "And then there will be plenty of time to massage your back once your belly is large and swollen."

"Why are you leaving at all?" I forced myself to take a deep breath. I didn't want Kwan to see me panic.

"They need me there."

"You're not their savior."

I tried to turn away, but Kwan held me against his chest. In Seoul I was always surprised at Kwan's protective love now that we were expecting our first child. I despised myself for not encouraging him more in his work for the Lord. I wanted to keep my husband here with me and forget about our pasts.

"I'm sorry," I admitted. "I just wish you didn't have to go." Kwan leaned over and kissed the top of my head. His hand rested on my abdomen, and he rubbed it gently.

"I'll be back soon. I'll take two months to help train some new leaders, then I'll return in time to see my wife grow large and plump. Think of all the children here eager to play with Auntie. You'll hardly notice that I'm missing." With his free hand, Kwan ran his fingers through my hair.

"What if something happens?" Away from Sanhe and the constant terror of surprise raids and repatriation, I grew even more dependent on my husband.

Kwan held me close. "God will take care of us." I cringed. *Didn't Father make the same promise so many years ago?*

I handed Kwan his passport and travel papers. Kwan leaned over and whispered to our child tucked away in my womb, "I love you, precious one."

You see, beloved daughter, that even as he was getting ready to leave in order to fulfill the work of the Lord, your father was thinking about you. Before you were born, he adored you – the precious daughter he would never meet.

BELOVED

"Let the beloved of the LORD rest secure in him, for he shields him all day long." Deuteronomy 33:12

With Kwan gone, there was nothing for me to do but rest and play with Mrs. Cho's rescued children. Even with my young compatriots vying for my attention, I fretted about Kwan for whole hours at a time. "You need to stop worrying," Mrs. Cho admonished. "Your baby knows when you're anxious." Mrs. Cho worked as a midwife before she started the orphanage. She promised Kwan that she would care for me with utmost skill and competence while he was away.

A month after his departure, Kwan wrote to tell me that he wouldn't be home by September as he first planned. In addition to training leaders for the Sanhe church, Kwan was asked to teach in an underground seminary for the entire border region of Jilin Province. He spent October and November out of phone contact. During that time I received one letter to assure me that he was still safe. In December, Kwan tried to return to Seoul, but by then his paperwork was expired, and he had to wait until he could come up with the appropriate bribe money to return home.

My first real contractions began on the second Thursday in January. Kwan sent me an international calling card so I could let him know when the time came, but Mrs. Cho guessed that the labor would be prolonged. She didn't want me to call my husband right away. When I finally gave birth on Saturday morning, Mrs. Cho cut the umbilical cord and held up a slimy, flailing little girl. After wrapping her in a small blanket, Mrs. Cho handed me my baby and walked toward the phone on the far side of the room. "And now you can call your husband."

Mrs. Cho found the calling card from Kwan and dialed the numbers. "It's connecting," she announced. My daughter began to turn her mouth toward me. As eager as I was to hear my husband's voice and tell him about our precious baby girl, I also wished Mrs. Cho would show me what I was supposed to do with a hungry newborn.

After nearly a minute, Mrs. Cho hung up the phone. "No answer." When she saw my daughter rubbing her cheek against my chest, she laughed. "A healthy appetite!" After several failed attempts, Mrs. Cho finally succeeded in attaching my baby to my breast.

"Are those tears of happiness or sorrow?" Mrs. Cho asked as I nursed my daughter for the first time.

I couldn't explain to my elderly benefactress the emotions I was experiencing. I was exhausted from my three-day labor and surprised that my daughter didn't look anything like the other infants I cared for. I never saw a baby so fresh from the womb before. I didn't expect my daughter to have such a skeletal frame or pointed skull, and I could only wonder why her skin was covered with a fine layer of soft gray fuzz.

I swallowed the lump in my throat and nodded. The joy of new life was clouded with overwhelming anxiety. I ached to present our firstborn to my husband, to smile as I watched Kwan hold her for the first time. Instead I wrapped my arms even more tightly around my daughter.

Mrs. Cho patted my head. "You should rest now," she instructed, leaving me alone to wonder if my child would ever meet her father face to face.

***

Mrs. Cho tried several more times that day and the next to call Kwan at the pastor's house in Sanhe. She never got through.

"Well," suggested Mrs. Cho after three days of silence, "perhaps they are so busy getting your husband's paperwork in order that they have no time for phone calls." She smiled at me. I clung to my daughter, staring into her eyes which looked so much like Kwan's.

"Father will be here soon," I whispered in her ear.

"What will you name her?"

Kwan and I never discussed baby names; we both assumed he would return home to Seoul months before the birth. I was about to beg for more time so Kwan could help me decide, but as our daughter stared at me with alert, black eyes, I knew what name to choose. "Ae-Cha," I declared, "so that everyone will know that she is our beloved daughter."

Mrs. Cho nodded in approval.

***

Days turned to weeks, and there was still no word from Kwan. I mailed him letters, even pictures of our growing child. Day and night I prayed for my husband's safety. When Ae-Cha was awake, I folded her hands together as if she were also asking God for her father's protection.

Mrs. Cho continued to bustle around the orphanage, letting me sleep in late, keeping the other children quiet so I could nap with Ae-Cha in the afternoons. In all respects, I was more like a boarder than a hired help. I was still weak from the delivery, and even though Ae-Cha slept well at night, I could barely find the strength for swaddling or diaper changing during the day.

I was resting with Ae-Cha in bed with me one afternoon when Mrs. Cho came in. "A letter," she announced. Her voice trembled. "From Sanhe."

I didn't recognize the handwriting on the envelope. Before opening it, I bundled up my sleeping daughter in her blanket and held her close against me. Her hair was thick and black. A good omen, I liked to think. I opened the letter and glanced at the signature. It was from the pastor's son in Sanhe.

Sister Chung-Cha,

I deeply regret that I must give you this difficult news. When your husband came to help me carry out my father's work in Sanhe, he knew that it was dangerous. It was nearly three weeks ago when I returned home and found the inside of my house ransacked. Your husband was home alone that day. I do not know where he is, although I am trying to find out. I would have written sooner, but your husband informed me of your condition and told me that if anything happened to him, I was not to contact you until well after your delivery date. I will write more as soon as I receive news.

Your servant,
Tong Dae-Jung

Mrs. Cho didn't have to read the letter to guess its nature. I buried my face in my daughter's silky hair and rocked her back and forth as I prayed for the man I had grown to love, the man I would never see again on this side of heaven.

OMEN

"From birth I was cast upon you; from my mother's womb you have been my God." Psalm 22:10

"It's your milk." Mrs. Cho repositioned her glasses on the knobby bridge of her nose. "Your supply has dried up."

I stroked Ae-Cha's cheek, murky from tear stains. She gazed up at me, her eyes swollen from crying and darkened by sleeplessness. Ae-Cha had been awake since midnight, kicking her legs and wailing while she pounded my breasts with tiny clenched fists.

"Already?" I exclaimed. "Why so soon?" I noticed that Ae-Cha's arms and legs remained bone-thin, but since her father was so skinny I didn't worry. When I couldn't console Ae-Cha after two hours of incessant screaming and dozens of failed attempts to nurse, I wrapped her in her blanket and took her across the hall to Mrs. Cho's bedroom.

"You've been too nervous." Mrs. Cho smacked her lips in Ae-Cha's face to distract my daughter from her hunger pains. I thought back to my childhood in Hasambong, when the empty ache of starvation robbed me of sleep on so many countless nights.

"How could I stop worrying?" What was I to do? Kwan disappeared nearly two months ago. I hadn't received any word from him, or the pastor's son, or anyone else in Sanhe since I first learned he was missing. I didn't know if my husband was dead or alive, healthy or broken. I clung to our daughter with zealous affection, but had no energy left to nourish her physical body.

I forced myself to believe that my love alone could shield Ae-Cha from whatever future lay ahead of us. Realizing that she might never meet her father, I vowed to love my daughter with the devotion and fervor of two parents. I slept with Ae-Cha by my side and carried her nearly every moment of the day, refusing to let even Mrs. Cho hold her. Feeling Ae-Cha's velvety skin against mine, her tiny fingers caressing my face as she explored her world, I was certain that I could live through one more day without giving in to panic or despair.

There was nothing I could do for Kwan from where I was, and so I wrapped Ae-Cha up within the four walls of my maternal adoration, vowing to do everything in my power to keep my daughter healthy and safe. I never let the other children play around her, terrified that they would pass on some horrific disease, or trip and crush her skull, or say something unkind that would scar her subconscious forever.

Whenever I nursed Ae-Cha, I felt my love and energy flow into her being. Mrs. Cho told me that a healthy baby only eats every four or five hours, but during the day Ae-Cha didn't let even an hour go by before turning her head to me with an irresistible expression. I loved the way Ae-Cha gazed at me while she nursed. With Ae-Cha at my breast, it seemed easier to believe that God truly did hear my prayers for Kwan and would bring him home to us.

Unfortunately, that peaceful bond I shared with Ae-Cha wasn't destined to last. With a sympathetic nod, Mrs. Cho handed me a bottle of formula that she prepared for my daughter. I held it up to Ae-Cha's eager lips. She began sucking loudly, occasionally letting out contented coos while warm, synthetic milk oozed out of the corners of her mouth.

I looked away. My husband was either locked in a Chinese jail cell, or his body was decaying in some make-shift grave. And all I wanted to do was cry because I could no longer nurse our child.

NIGHTMARE

"Anyone who loves his son or daughter more than me is not worthy of me." Matthew 10:37

I never expected to find myself back in Sanhe again. Desperate to find my husband, I traveled back to Jilin Province with Ae-Cha slung up on my back in search for news about Kwan.

I went to Pastor Tong's home, wondering if his son was still free in Sanhe or if he was imprisoned like his father. I only saw their home once before when Kwan and I tarried too far on one of our evening walks. Standing on the front porch under the cover of nightfall, I lifted my hand. I felt the heavy weight of Ae-Cha's sleeping form on my back and was comforted by her tranquil breathing. Mustering some remnant courage, I tapped once on the door. It opened before I could knock a second time.

"Hurry!" hissed a man. The inside of the house was so dark that I could hardly see the figure in front of me.

"Who are you?" I asked.

"Don't you recognize me?" Once the door was closed, the man struck a match. The small flame flickered across a familiar face.

"Moses?"

He put his finger to his lips and scowled. "Shh." He touched the match to the wick of a candle. "No one is supposed to know who I am."

Ae-Cha woke up in my backpack and began to fuss.

"If you'll allow me." Moses lifted Ae-Cha out of my sling. With surprising gentleness, he cradled her in his arm.

"She looks so much like her father." Moses wiggled his finger in front of Ae-Cha's face and made cooing sounds.

"Where is Kwan?" I asked, keeping a close watch on my daughter, who smiled at her new friend.

Ignoring my question, Moses turned his back to me and carried Ae-Cha into the other room. "I'll go fix her a bottle."

"I want to see my husband," I called after him.

"Very soon." Moses' cheerful voice seemed far too loud for a man who was hiding. A moment later he returned without Ae-Cha.

"Where is my daughter?" My entire body tensed in fear. "What did you do with her?"

Moses narrowed his eyes, his carefree manner replaced with the brusque callousness that came so easily to him as a prison guard. "Did you tell them?"

"Tell who?"

"The world. Or did you forget as soon as you were out of harm's reach?"

"Where is my daughter?" I repeated as Ae-Cha whimpered in the other room.

"A child only gets in the way." Moses blocked the path to my baby.

"She needs me." I struggled to get by.

"You can't go to her." Moses grabbed my shoulders and wouldn't let me go. "There is too much work for you to do here. The underground church needs you."

"I didn't come to save the church," I insisted. "I only came to find out about my husband."

"Kwan is dead." Moses' voice was lifeless and flat. "And we will all die as well if you don't stop playing house and help us."

From the other room Ae-Cha's cries grew louder. I tried again to go toward her. "You must know that you can't take a child with you to serve our people." Moses squeezed my shoulder so hard it forced me to the ground. I cried out in surprise as much as in pain. "Why did you bring her here?" I gasped when I saw the revolver in Moses' hand. Ae-Cha was now wailing, her high-pitched shrieks making even Moses wince. He shook his head. "You should have never brought her here."

"Please." I wondered what bribe I could possibly offer. "Ae-Cha needs me."

"She needs you?" Moses raised a thick black eyebrow. "Or do you need her?"

I tried to push the National Security agent aside, but he caught my shirt and spun me around. "Let me go!" Moses held my wrists in front of me while I tried to claw at his chest and screamed Ae-Cha's name. Candlelight flickered across the room, making our struggling shadows dance across the wall.

"I can't have the two of you going on like this." Moses clucked his tongue. "It is a pity, really. She might have grown up to make a good agent for the underground church one day."

"Let me go!" I pleaded as Moses handcuffed my wrists to a table leg. "I'll do anything."

Moses looked at me sadly and shook his head.

"I know, righteous daughter." Moses loaded his gun and pointed it toward the direction of my daughter's terrified screams. "That's why you should have never had a child." With a shrug of his shoulders, Moses pulled the trigger.

***

The back of my nightgown was soaked with sweat. It clung to my clammy skin. I heard Ae-Cha crying next to me, but I couldn't move, as if I were still restrained by the handcuffs from my nightmare.

A moment later Mrs. Cho rushed into my room wearing her nightclothes and carrying a bottle. She flung on the light and then swooped up my daughter. Ae-Cha smacked loudly at her formula. I wiped the sweat-drenched hair out of my eyes.

"I'm still in Seoul?"

Mrs. Cho frowned while she studied me. "A dream?"

I nodded my head, staring at the wet spot on my pillow where I had been lying.

"An omen, perhaps?" Mrs. Cho pressed. "Something about your husband?"

I shook my head and reached out to take my daughter, whose eyelids already started to droop as the warm milk filled her stomach.

"No." I stroked Ae-Cha's flawless face and kissed her forehead. "It was just a dream." I forced conviction into my voice where there was none. "A silly nightmare, and nothing more."

MESSENGER

"By oppression and judgment he was taken away. And who can speak of his descendants?" Isaiah 53:8

Mrs. Cho stood at the entrance to my room. For a moment she watched with a half-smile as Ae-Cha batted at a blue baby rattle in my hand. Ae-Cha was growing plump now that she was taking a bottle, and her strong legs kicked happily as she sat in my lap. After a short silence, Mrs. Cho cleared her throat. "There is a visitor for you. From Sanhe."

I stood up and swept my hair behind my ears. I cradled Ae-Cha in front of me, not quite certain if I was protecting her or if she was shielding me. Mrs. Cho herded all the other children toward the upstairs playroom. I took a deep breath, surprisingly composed. Even if the messenger brought bad news about Kwan, at least the dreadful uncertainty and waiting would be over.

As Mrs. Cho receded to the back stairway with the last of the children, I stared at the messenger who came to bring me word from Sanhe. The gray-haired man was even more bent than when I last saw him. He stared at the carpet in front of my feet.

"Mr. Kim?" Alone with my betrayer, with Mrs. Cho and the other children upstairs and out of hearing range, I wished for somewhere to hide. Even though I never yet let her out of my sight, I regretted not sending my daughter to the playroom with the others, as if Mr. Kim's very presence had the power to harm her.

Mr. Kim refused to sit down or enter into the living room but stood at the threshold boring holes into the floor with his eyes. He shuffled his feet once, cleared his throat, and remained silent.

"Why did you come here?" I asked, more out of surprise than rudeness. Mr. Kim clasped, opened, and re-clasped his hands in front of him.

"Do you have news of Kwan?" I finally demanded, unable to endure the silence.

"Dead." Mr. Kim's voice was barely audible. "Last month in the Longjing jail." He sniffed and coughed, and I realized that his words only confirmed what my heart already knew with certainty.

I waited for Mr. Kim to offer some word of sympathy or remorse as I ran my hand repeatedly over my daughter's ears, as if I might forever shield her from this news. "There is more." Mr. Kim shifted his weight.

"What else could there be?" Ae-Cha was heavy in my arms. Overwhelmed with weariness. I longed to take Ae-Cha to bed with me and sleep for days.

Mr. Kim squinted his eyes, as if the light in the room was painful to him. "Moses was arrested."

The words hung in the air between us. Reminding myself to continue inhaling and exhaling, I willed away the image of Kwan's broken body finally giving in to the maltreatment of the Longjing jail.

"Arrested?" I repeated. "By whom?" I couldn't fathom the implications of Moses' capture and wished even more that Mr. Kim would leave me and my daughter alone.

"National Security Agency." My exhausted mind was spinning. If Moses was caught by the Chinese, perhaps he could continue to hide his identity as a Korean official. Since Pyongyang had him instead, I didn't want to imagine the horrors that would befall him.

"Why are you telling me?" I remembered how strictly Mr. Kim guarded safe-house secrets in Sanhe.

"I saw Moses in January." Ae-Cha made gurgling noises and tugged at the hair that hung down in my eye. "He knew he was under suspicion. He told me that if I heard of his arrest, I was to find you." For the first time, Mr. Kim looked up, not at my face, but at the smiling baby I held in my arms.

"You know his identity." Mr. Kim whispered, as if Mrs. Cho or even the orphans upstairs might one day be interrogated by the National Security Agency and forced to confess what they overheard in the drawing room. "And so you're the only one who could save Moses now."

"What can I do?" I regretted that Moses ever told me who he was. Didn't I already know enough of torture and raids and prison cells?

"There is a high-ranking Party official, a secret Christian worker. He's the only man with the power to save Moses." I was glad at least to hear there was some hope for my father's friend. "But he cannot help a man who remains nameless."

"You want me to tell you Moses' identity?" After what took place in the mountains of Jilin Province, I could never trust Mr. Kim with such information.

Mr. Kim shook his head. "I would not accept that burden for all the yuan in Asia." Mr. Kim stared back down at the floor. Did he realize how his allusion to bribery sounded in my ears?

"Then I still don't understand. How can I help Moses from here in Seoul?"

Mr. Kim stared unsmiling at Ae-Cha. "You can do nothing from Seoul," he declared.

SURROGATE

"Kings will be your foster fathers, and their queens your nursing mothers." Isaiah 49:23

"And so you must return to Sanhe?" Mrs. Cho crossed her arms against her chest and gazed at me over her spectacles.

"This man has saved hundreds of believers." I recited the argument I rehearsed so often over the past two days.

Mrs. Cho stared at Ae-Cha who had fallen asleep just a moment earlier in my arms, a pacifier dangling precariously from her open mouth.

"If you were returning to Jilin Province to find your husband, I would perhaps understand." Mrs. Cho had been separated from her husband decades earlier during the Peninsula War. She gazed at a photograph of a young man on the bookshelf behind us. "But for a man you hardly know? To put yourself in such danger …"

I couldn't explain to Mrs. Cho why I had to go back to help Moses, the hero of my childhood fantasies, the friend of my father, the son of one of my dearest companions.

"I have no choice," I concluded. "Fate's already made this decision for me."

"Not fate perhaps," Mrs. Cho reminded me and looked out the window at the setting sun. Faint wisps of pink and pale orange outlined the early spring clouds. I didn't tell my benefactress that I was not only planning to return to Sanhe but would have to cross the border into North Korea one last time. Mrs. Cho pursed her thin lips.

"You know I can't take Ae-Cha with me."

As soon as I spoke the words, Mrs. Cho's sighed loudly. She studied my face. "A difficult decision." Suddenly self-conscious,

I wondered if Mrs. Cho heard my cries these past two nights. "But perhaps a wise one," the elderly woman reassured me. I tried to think of something other than the perfect, angelic form cradled against my chest, her cheek wet from drool, her lips open in a contented half-smile.

Without saying anything, Mrs. Cho took my daughter from my arms. Ae-Cha grunted, scrunched up her face into an angry pout, and then fell back into a blissful, sleepy stupor as Mrs. Cho nuzzled my baby's cheek with her nose.

"I will watch your Ae-Cha until your return." Mrs. Cho kissed my daughter on the forehead.

I looked away, longing to run to my bed so that dreamless sleep might save me from this tortuous parting. Even though I already memorized what I was going to say next, I had to force out each syllable.

"If I don't return," I bit my quivering lip until I was able to continue, "I would like you to raise Ae-Cha."

At first Mrs. Cho raised her hand as if to swat away my inauspicious remark. But instead, she caressed Ae-Cha's thick hair and declared, "You have my word."

Unable to continue watching my daughter as she dozed so contentedly in another woman's arms, I retreated to my room while Mrs. Cho sang Ae-Cha a lilting lullaby.

I had never heard the melody before.

PARTING

"Do not be afraid of what you are about to suffer ... Be faithful, even to the point of death, and I will give you the crown of life."
Revelation 2:10

Once my travel papers to Jilin Province arrived, I spent more time alone in my room, leaving Mrs. Cho to watch after Ae-Cha. I told myself that it would be better for Ae-Cha if she got used to Mrs. Cho's care, but in reality it was harder for me to spend time with my daughter at all when I knew I had to leave her so soon. The night before my departure, Mrs. Cho carried Ae-Cha into my room.

"You haven't finished yet?" Mrs. Cho glanced at the journal on the desk in front of me

"I'm almost done." I closed the book and stared at Mrs. Cho. She was old enough to be Ae-Cha's great-grandmother but held Ae-Cha with the same care as if she herself had borne her. I wondered how many mothers my daughter would lose in her lifetime.

"I only regret she won't remember me," I muttered.

Mrs. Cho pursed her lips. "You shouldn't speak like that." Her voice cracked in spite of her admonition.

I looked at the book in front of me. "There is so much history. So much sorrow. I wish she didn't have to learn it this way." Mrs. Cho nodded, although she knew very little of my past as the daughter of a Christian traitor. "There are so many things that I hoped to tell her face to face. Not like this."

Mrs. Cho placed Ae-Cha into my arms and sat on my bed. She nodded toward the leather-bound journal. "I will keep your story safe while you are gone. Ae-Cha will want to know as much about her mother as she can." I wondered if my benefactress had the same premonitions as I did about the journey ahead of me. After an uncomfortable silence, Mrs. Cho asked, "You are still sure that you must go?"

I nodded, clearing my throat before I could speak. "The choice isn't my own."

"How long do you expect to be gone?"

I couldn't tell Mrs. Cho what I was already certain of in my heart. Unwilling to answer her question, I looked again at the journal on my desk. "I wrote to her as if I would never see her again." I gazed at my daughter. She looked so much like her father I sometimes felt as though I was staring into the face of Kwan's ghost. "If I return," I finally faltered, "I'll have no reason to hold on to this journal. I'll tell her these stories myself when she is old enough."

"And if you are ... delayed?" Mrs. Cho asked.

"You must give it to her when you think best." Forgive me, dear and precious Ae-Cha! Forgive me for the choices that robbed you of your mother at such a young and tender age.

"Please." I turned my face away from the contented girl in my arms. "This is more than I can endure." Mrs. Cho took Ae-Cha back from me and rocked my daughter in her arms. I motioned toward the journal. "I'm almost done. I need to finish before morning."

Mrs. Cho looked at me with moist eyes. Did she sense what was about to transpire? "Do you want me to wake Ae-Cha up in the morning to see you off?"

I turned my back to the elderly woman and shook my head. "I don't think I would be able to stand it."

"Good-night, then, righteous daughter." Mrs. Cho couldn't keep her voice from breaking. She carried Ae-Cha out and closed the door behind her. The soft click echoed through my empty room.

I fingered the leather journal. I still hadn't written any inscription on first page. Taking a deep breath, I let my tears splash onto the paper as I scrolled:

To my precious Ae-Cha,
so you will always know that you are
my beloved daughter.